Good Pussy Bad Pussy

Rachel's Tale

A. Aimee

Winchester, UK
Washington, USA

First published by Bedroom Books, 2013
Bedroom Books is an imprint of John Hunt Publishing Ltd., Laurel House, Station Approach,
Alresford, Hants, SO24 9JH, UK
office1@jhpbooks.net
www.johnhuntpublishing.com
www.bedroom-books.com

For distributor details and how to order please visit the 'Ordering' section on our website.

ISBN: 978 1 78279 084 6

A CIP catalogue record for this book is available from the British Library.

Design: Stuart Davies

Printed in the USA by Edwards Brothers Malloy

We operate a distinctive and ethical publishing philosophy in all
areas of our business, from our global network of authors to
production and worldwide distribution.

CONTENTS

PART I

THE FRENCH RIVIERA

I was incredibly horny and told myself it was true love, great passion, high romance, so I left my husband and four-year old son in Amsterdam and went to Nice with Stefan. It was almost the end of August. I had a lot to learn.

We had been in Nice a few days when Stefan said, "Tonight we're going to meet Albert. Go get your hair done."

He put money in my hand.

"I'll wait for you on the beach. When you're done, we'll go buy you some new clothes."

So I was finally going to meet the big man. It was about time. I was really curious. Stefan never talked very much, but when he did Albert always turned up in the conversation.

After I got my hair done, Stefan took me shopping. He took me to the expensive boutiques on the Avenue Jean Medecin. We went into a shop with Yves Saint Laurent dresses and Gucci bags in the window. A glamorous woman waited on us. Stefan told her what kind of a dress he was looking for. She eyed me for size and came out with an absolutely stunning creamy white dress. It had a tight-fitting bodice with thin straps and a loose soft flowing skirt.

Stefan nodded, "Go try it on."

It fit perfectly and looked divine. I couldn't believe it was me. I had always wanted to look like that. When I came out to show Stefan he said, "That will be ok for tonight, but now you need some more clothes."

He bought me sexy lace underwear, new shoes and a bag to match. Designer jeans, a slew of t-shirts, a new bikini, skinny white pants and a white jacket. I couldn't believe how much money he was spending. Everything was packed up and we went back to the hotel.

"Go put your make-up on," Stefan said, "we're going to have dinner with Albert."

I took my time. It was hard to get used to the feeling of luxury, clothes, money, the Riviera. I felt guilty about running out on my husband and son and having a good time.

Stefan was satisfied with the way I looked. When we got to the door of our suite he said, "Give me your panties."

I took them off. They were the beautiful new lace ones he'd just bought me. He put them in his pocket.

"Let's go," he said.

Down on the street, a limousine was waiting for us. The chauffeur opened the door and we got in. As we drove along, Stefan put his arm around me and kissed me on the neck.

"I want you to do whatever Albert wants," he said softly in my ear even though the chauffeur could not possibly hear us through the glass that separated him from us. "Do you understand?"

"What do you mean?" I asked in surprise.

"Well... he may not want anything... but then again, he might want to bed you. He has before with other women I've known."

"But..." I started to say.

Stefan put his fingers to my lips.

He was blond, muscular and divinely beautiful. I was madly in love with him or so I thought.

"Don't ask me why. If you really feel as you say about me, you'll do what I ask."

I trembled all over. This was an unexpected turn of events. Not how I had imagined things would be. I'd never been to bed with a man I didn't know. Just like that.

But it was strange and exciting to be sitting on the backseat of a limousine in a marvelous dress with no panties on. Stefan put his hand up my dress. The moisture between my legs embarrassed me. We pulled up before a posh-looking restaurant but Stefan did not remove his hand. Instead he kissed me long and passionately on the mouth.

wished piercingly that I was home again, safe from this adventure. The ache inside was hard and cold and I felt panic.

Albert came out on the balcony with a drink in his hand. "You must not catch cold my dear. Come inside." I was positive he knew exactly what I was feeling.

Inside the space was bare, open, and minimalistic, almost Zen in nature and appearance. A single bonsai, exquisite and proud on a tiny polished black table. A large smooth round stone in the corner.

He put on some quiet music and took me in his arms to dance. He was teasing me, testing me, playing with me. There was something almost ruthless about his debonair manner. And even though I was trying to act cool, I was all fluttery inside.

"Why did you leave your husband for Stefan?" he asked me.

"Oh I don't know... I just couldn't help myself."

"Ahh..." He said. "So the blood in your veins runs very hot, is that it?" He took my chin in his hands and forced me to look up at him. He examined my face slowly and smiled, not unkindly. I felt shy and full of strange desire at the same time. When he seemed satisfied, he led me over to one of the few armchairs in the sparely furnished room. It was a large and comfortable.

"Let's see if you really are as warm as you are beautiful."

He took off his jacket and loosened his tie.

"Make yourself comfortable Rachel."

I sat down in the huge armchair, my heart pounding in my chest.

He got down on his knees and positioned himself right between my legs. Then he leaned forward and kissed me on the mouth, slow and easy, just exploring. I didn't feel aroused, only afraid. But there was no turning back now. I had chosen this myself. This was the real, raw adventure I'd been dreaming of.

But then I thought of Jan and the life I'd left behind and my heart skipped a beat. Did I know what I was doing? Suddenly my old life seemed so much more attractive... or maybe I was just longing for the safety of the known. You could do the same thing with many men. What was the difference? And then there was our child! My son! Why hadn't I seen it before? Did I have to lose him to realize how precious he was!

And what about Stefan? How could he just turn me over to another man like that, even if Albert was his mentor and hero? What was with him? What were they into? I shivered inside, realizing I didn't have a clue as to what I'd gotten myself into.

At that very moment, Albert began fondling my nipples just firmly enough to excite me. I didn't resist, nor did I participate. I just let it happen, as if I was watching him and myself from some far away place. This was such a new experience for me; being touched by a man I'd never met before. I didn't quite know what to think or feel. But Albert was so powerful and attractive that I found it strangely thrilling to feel him touching me so I let myself settle back into the chair.

He understood my body language immediately because he let go of my nipples and lifted my legs expertly and placed them one on each arm of the chair so I was spread eagle before him. I stiffened in surprise, remembering I had no panties on. He went down on me, not waiting for my consent, but tasting me slowly and making me wet. Oh my God, I thought... was this me? Was I really doing this?

But yes I was... and then...

Oh my, oh my...

I heard myself moaning at the thrill of his tongue touching me.

He was good... goodness he was good...

He removed his lips from and put his fingers up me with a gentle firmness that bespoke a knowingness of women and years of experience. I gasped. He came up to me again and began kissing me on the mouth, keeping his fingers in me at the same time. I moaned as he kept on touching me knowingly, kissing me and bearing down on me. There was no resisting him now. And I felt myself opening even wider under his expert touch.

"You're..." I mumbled not knowing how to react, confused by the intense pleasure I was feeling.

"I want to see you come," he murmured in my ear, his fingers emerging slowly from inside me and again playing gently with my innermost lips, caressing them ever so softly. Ahh... The softness of his touch was exquisite, so exquisite. And he waited as I sighed even more deeply and he continued to caress me with such perfect gentleness until he knew that I wanted him too, wanted him to see me surrender completely to his touch.

Then he went down on me again, this time even more slowly, kissing my very wet pussy and doing things to me with his tongue that I'd never experienced before.

I heard myself gasping again with pleasure.

He was a man who could take me exactly where he wanted me to go. And he did. I was defenseless against the tide of liquid desire he released in me. And then I felt it, the confusion of emotions, the rush of ecstasy, the warmth, the wetness. I heard myself moaning and I grabbed his hair – I was nearing the point of no return. I cried out... shaking and trembling, exactly as he knew I would... exactly... and I was there, precisely where he wanted me to be... there as the tide of liquid desire swept me away... and I disappeared happily, ecstatically into the ecstasy of the most amazing, shuddering climax.

No man had ever made me feel like that before. Ever!

When I opened my eyes, my fingers were twisted in Albert's hair. I would have pushed him away, but he didn't give me time. He grabbed me and pulled me up. Now he too was aroused. There was no mistaking the hungry look on his aristocratic face, a look mixed with satisfaction. Now he wanted me too. He led me to the bedroom.

"Take off your dress."

I did as he said. Trembling and bold at the same time.

He undressed and came to me on the low bed. I was wet and ready. He entered me and I gasped, not expecting him to be so hard. He held my hands down and rose above me. There was something strangely magnetic and powerful about him, something I'd never seen in any man before. He grabbed my hair and pulled my head back, my body bending to his will. He was approaching his climax.

"Tell me, do you want it?"

He looked me deep in the eyes, his gaze penetrating me.

When I didn't answer, he said it again, "Tell me, do you want it?"

He had this intense, one-pointed quality about him and I felt myself being drawn into his passion "Yes," I murmured softly, "yes."

He thrust himself deeper into me. "Say please."

And then he paused, breaking his rhythm and moving in me slowly and sensually until I felt that tide of liquid desire rising in me again. Oh my, oh my! Again!

"Say it!" He moved faster, deeper.

"Say it!"

And I felt it; the liquid tide was gaining momentum – again – and moving, moving, moving... ready to sweep me away until I heard myself crying, "Yes please, please!"

And then he did sweep me away with a fierceness and intensity that did not stop until we both shuddered and came at exactly the same moment. Then he lay on top of me for a long time, his face turned away.

When at last he looked at me with those deep penetrating eyes of his, I felt so many strange emotions.

* * *

When I got back to our suite at the hotel, I was relieved that Stefan wasn't there. I didn't want to face him just then. I wanted to be alone. So much had happened. I needed to sort out my feelings. I had gone through so many changes in one evening. Albert said very little after his first explosion inside me, but there had been a change in him. After we lay still for a long while on the low bed, he made love to me again. But the second time was so different from the first, so tender and gentle, showing me another side of this incredible man. And later, when he drove me home with the wind in his face, he was silent and I liked him for it.

But by the time he left me at the door to the hotel, he was the same again as he was in the beginning.

"I hope our little princess has enjoyed herself," he whispered in my ear and left.

When I got back to our suite, I closed the door and leaned against it, my legs trembled so. Then I went to the bedroom and lay down fully dressed on the bed, overwhelmed by what had just happened and by what I had just done. There was no denying it; this was the real raw adventure I'd been dreaming of, but what I hadn't expected was that it would trigger such powerful emotions in me. Albert was such an incredible man. I'd never met anyone like him before and didn't know what to feel or think. Our meeting had been so... Was this the beginning of my liberation or enslavement? Oh where oh where had good pussy, bad pussy just taken me?

Albert!

Stefan!

Good pussy bad pussy!

What was going on?

What was happening to me?

All I knew for sure was that I'd experienced a depth of passion I'd never tasted before – and with a man I'd only just met.

I didn't know what to think and drifted off to sleep.

Much later, I heard the bedroom door open and knew it was

Stefan. I didn't want to face him so I pretended I was sleeping. I heard him moving around the room. He didn't turn on the light or try to wake me. Instead he came over to me and gently raised my dress. I was lying on my stomach and he lowered himself down on me. I was still wet from Albert, so he entered me easily.

"Oh Rachel," he whispered tenderly in my ear, "if only you knew how sorry I am. If only you could understand, I couldn't prevent tonight from happening."

I was stunned. He had never been like that before, never showed me that he cared – at least not like that. Before he'd always carefully kept his distance, closed in upon himself like a beautiful oyster. But as I felt him growing in me, he was holding me tighter than he had ever done before. Loving me as I had hoped he would, finally, when I thought I might be through with him. Thought I might be through with him for giving me so nonchalantly to his best friend. But how could I be? How could I be through with the man I had wanted so desperately, right up until that very day? The man who had swept me off my feet with his silent beauty? I might have been confused by it all, but deep down in my heart of hearts, I knew I couldn't resist him – at least not for long. Not for more than a second or two. So I let myself glide away and be swallowed up by the force of his passion. Only in the dark, when he thought I was half asleep could Stefan reveal his true feelings for me, only after he had coolly given me to his best friend and mentor, the incredible man who had just possessed me so utterly and completely.

* * *

When I woke up the next morning, Stefan was already out in the bathroom shaving. He came out smiling and said, "Come on Rachel, hurry up and get dressed. I am going to take you sailing."

No reference to the past night. He was just like he always was, cool, calm, and tightly closed upon himself. Not a trace of emotion on his beautiful face. My beloved Adonis went back to the bathroom, his face only half shaved, the other half still white with shaving cream. If I didn't get out of bed right away and start dressing, I'd have to make a scene and leave him. But his lovemaking and the events of the night before had confused me. I had to wait and see. And besides, I'd had never been sailing before. I got up and got dressed.

Stefan and I grabbed a taxi at the Place Massena and drove out along the coast on the Lower Corniche. The day was warm and sunny. We got off at Villefranche, a fantastic bay and harbor, which I immediately fell in love with. We walked down to the quays and sat at an outdoor café and had coffee and croissants. Stefan pointed across the water and told me that all the rich people lived over there on Cap Ferrat. I could see the hanging gardens and beautiful houses. Stefan reminded me that Albert had a house on Cap Ferrat too.

We spent the day sailing on a sea of blue glass.

But underneath the surface of amazing calm, I was volcano of conflicting thoughts and emotions. I simply couldn't figure out what the deal was with Stefan and Albert. Here I was, Stefan's girlfriend of the moment, and Stefan had just let Albert, his great hero and mentor, sleep with me, his woman. He even mentioned right before it happened that Albert had slept with other women he'd been with. What was with him? Didn't it bother him? And what about me? Didn't it bother me? Even though I vaguely thought it should, when I thought about the incredible night I just had with Albert, I realized there was no easy answer to that question either. Simply because making love with Albert had been such an extraordinary experience. Up until that night, I'd thought sex with Stefan was the best thing I'd ever experienced. But it turned out that sex with Albert was even better. It was simply out of this world. Way beyond anything I'd ever experienced before. The man had awakened this incredible tide of liquid desire in me that I didn't even know existed. And the experience had been so powerful that it overshadowed everything else. So honestly no, the fact that Stefan had shared me with Albert didn't bother me either.

All I knew for sure was that just the thought of how deeply Albert had touched me, made me tremble all over. And I couldn't help but wonder how Albert felt about our encounter too. Was I just one more woman in a long line of women to him or had he felt the power of our coming together the way I did? There was just something about it, something about the intensity of our meeting that had blown me away.

So there I was, confused maybe, but feeling so very, very alive. Wondering what would happen next. But not much did... at least not for the next few days. In fact, the following days passed quietly enough. Stefan and I slept late and went down to the beach. We didn't see Albert. Sometimes Stefan left me alone on the beach for a few hours to do some business, which I didn't mind at all. In fact I liked lying on the beach all alone, savoring the feeling of liquid desire in my loins. Stefan and I never talked about Albert either or about the night I'd spent with him or about anything that was emotionally difficult. Nor did we talk about the future or what would happen to us. We took long walks in Nice, along the Promenade Des Anglais, looking at all the big hotels and the crowds on the beach. We explored the Old Town, which seemed vaguely Italian and we ate the famous bouillabaisse there.

Then one day, out of the blue, my parents called and said they were coming to Nice, the very next day. I was so surprised. Of course they knew I was in Nice, but I didn't in my wildest dreams expect to see them there. But they said they were on their way from New York to Israel to meet some friends and decided to stop over in Nice for a day to see me.

So the next evening, Jerry and Isabel arrived and I discovered that despite the fact that my life was in turmoil, I was really looking forward to seeing them. Waiting at the airport, I made up my mind that I was going to try to be honest with them about what was going on in my life. I just had the feeling that if I had the nerve to tell them the truth, my mother in particular would understand me. I guess I felt this way because my mother was a very elegant lady who always seemed to know more than I expected. She'd been married once before she met my father and sometimes made references to a past that didn't sound exactly typical. Her flair, her manner, her way of dressing spoke discreetly of a worldliness that the rest of us didn't possess. She was very different from my father who was just a regular hard-working guy with a kind heart who was getting more and more sentimental with age. I was his only child so he really had a soft spot for me. I also had an older, half-sister, Marlene who was eight years older than I and was my mother's daughter from her first marriage. I never got to know Marlene that well because she was so much older than I was. And besides, we were as different as day and night. Unlike me, she'd never really tested her limits or been a wild child, but rather followed the straight and narrow path. When she graduated from college, she married a doctor, and settled down. She lived on Long Island with her husband and two children and once in a while sent me emails with pictures of her well-dressed family.

I saw my parents coming through into the arrival hall. My father looked older and my mother looked tired, but when they saw me, they brightened and came rushing forward.

"Rachel! Why Rachel darling, don't you look beautiful! How are you?" They both said, kissing and hugging me. My mother was looking at the elegant white suit I had on. Her right eyebrow arched ever so slightly as if to say – this is a change!

When we got to their hotel room, my mother went to the bathroom to freshen up. My father stretched and yawned and then put his arms around me, his sentimental side showing its head. There were tiny tears in his beady brown eyes. But they still sparkled like they used to do when I was little and had been particularly naughty.

"Oh Rachel, it's so good to see you. Am I going to hear about one of your adventures again? Aren't you a mother now with a beautiful son?" He sighed, let go of me and sat down tiredly in the big armchair. Then he smiled. "But you know I could never get angry with you, could I? All I can ever see is the mischievous, little green-eyed girl you once were. I guess you will always be my little girl. After all, how many daughters do I have? Ah Rachel... I like to think you take after me!"

My mother came out of the bathroom and when she saw the tears in my father's eyes, she said gently, "Remember Jerry, we promised each other not to get upset. Now go in and freshen up so we can go down and have dinner. I'm famished."

My father disappeared into the bathroom.

"Gee Mom," I sighed, "you look great, you always do. What's your secret?"

"You know I only wish we had a few days to talk, really talk." My mother looked at me. "I've experienced things I've never told you about and now that you're 35, you're old enough to understand."

Then she examined the white suit I was wearing and added, "What a stunning suit this is... I've never seen you wear anything like this before. Are you really here in Nice all by yourself?"

"What do you think?"

"I figured as much," she said and signed. "I only hope that whatever you have to tell us will not weigh too heavily upon your father. He's not as strong as he used to be."

"I really don't want to upset him, or you either, but I really do want to talk."

My father heard my last remark as he came out of the bathroom.

"Talk? Of course we're going to talk. I want to hear exactly what's going on. Do you think I came all the way to Nice just to look at the beach? Now let's go down and eat and you can tell us everything."

As soon as the waiter left with our orders, my mother started, "So you walked out on Jan and Daniel to come to Nice with whom?"

"He must be something," my father said and sighed. "You know I've never said a word against Jan, even though I wished you had married someone who lived a little closer to New York, or who at least had a little more money. But done is done and I've never complained. And now you are going to tell me things aren't working out?"

"Yes," I said, tears welling up in my eyes. I couldn't help it I started crying. "I'm so confused."

"Come, come Rachel," my father patted my hand rather ineffectively, "there must be more to it than that. You can tell us."

"Well," I said slowly, "As far as appearances go, things were pretty okay. It was just…"

"Just what?" my mother said, looking at me rather sharply.

That only made me cry more.

"It was just…" I said again slowly.

"Just what?" my mother repeated more slowly and more gently.

"Well just…" I was struggling to find the words, "I felt like I was suffocating. Like my life was going down the tube! It was all just so meaningless."

My parents were silent, both looking at me with their kind eyes, so I rushed on. "Not only was our life together such a bore, but Jan is so…"

I paused, not knowing how to explain.

"So what?" my father asked.

"So mean and cold – and so small-minded!"

There I'd said it! I'd blurted it out. Jan was a bore, an asshole. My life sucked.

Now that it was out, I rushed on. "I mean our life together was just so uninteresting… I don't know if you can understand but I just felt like I couldn't breathe anymore," I paused for a moment and then plunged on. "I just couldn't figure out what I was living for... And Jan never really saw me anyway. He just took me for granted, like I was a piece of furniture or something! It seemed like my only job was to make him happy!"

There it was.

My truth. What a relief to finally say it. Up until then, I hadn't fully understood it myself. But now that I said it, there it was, lying quietly on the table before us. Like a smooth, round stone, silent and hard. My truth! My life was a bore! My husband was a jerk! Hearing my own words was such a revelation.

"It was just so frustrating, having a small child and all that and Jan being so closed in upon himself. In the end it was just the same old, same old routine every day. It was like I didn't feel like a real person anymore." I cried some more. "I know this sounds really stupid, but it was just such a drag... In the end, it was like I didn't exist."

"Ah Rachel," my mother sighed and said thoughtfully, "This is something that happens to many women your age. Suddenly your youth is gone and you think, is this really it? Is this really my life? Is this all there is to it? It happened to me too so I know how scary it can be. So many of us go through this... one way or another. What it really means is that it's time for you to find something interesting to do with your life, whether or not you stay with Jan. It's high time you start making a life for yourself! But Rachel darling, it doesn't mean you have to leave your son, your precious child!"

"Oh I know," I said crying even more. "What a mess I've made of things. My poor baby! I miss him so much... I really do..." I blew my nose and then added, sniffing, "I probably wouldn't have left him if I hadn't met Stefan."

"So," my father said, fingering his napkin and looking down at the table, "you wanted to go to bed with this Stefan and instead of being like we used to be when we were young, you actually did go to bed with him. And you liked it very much."

Hearing these words from my father really surprised me. He never seemed to understand my generation before so this was really a change.

"How did you know?" I asked.

"Don't you think we know a little about sex too, my dear?"

"I just didn't think you could possibly understand what I've done. I feel like such a fool." I started to cry again.

"We all make mistakes, Rachel," my father said, "but that doesn't mean you abandon your child… Think about what you're doing, sweetheart! Is this guy Stefan worth it?"

It was true; I didn't know what to think.

There was a loaded silence. Then I said what I guessed we were all thinking, "So you think I should go back or what? I mean what would I do? Go back to Jan? Get a divorce?"

"How should we know Rachel? But for starters you could go back and have a talk with Jan," my father said. "I mean he is your husband – so why not tell him exactly what you just told us? Why not tell him the truth? Why not tell him how unhappy you are with your life."

"I don't know if I can – he's so hard to talk to."

"Well you could try. Don't you think you owe it to your son?"

I was grateful that the waiter came with our food. Not that I was hungry, but I needed a break, and time to assimilate what my parents said. Of course I had expected them to scold me, but did they really understand? Could they possibly understand how difficult living with Jan was and how dissatisfied I was with my life? And what about the whole sex thing? The whole good pussy bad pussy thing? Could they possibly understand how strong that drive was? And how it drove me to experiment and do things I couldn't possibly tell them about? Like sleeping with Stefan's best friend and loving it too? How could they understand when I hardly understood it myself! *Stefan! Albert! Good pussy bad pussy!* I didn't know what to make of it… or her.

All I knew for sure was that when I met Stefan, I just wanted to forget everything else about my life. All I wanted was to disappear down the rabbit hole into the ecstasy of our sexual encounters. Being with Stefan had made me feel so real again, so alive. There was just something about it that made me forget everything else. It was so deep, like total annihilation. I just loved it. I loved disappearing into the bliss. And when that happened, I didn't want my real life anymore. I didn't want to wake up anymore with a husband who was as cold as ice and always lost in his own worries. I just knew there had to be more to life than that. With Stefan it was different. When I was with him, all my frustrations disappeared into this shining passion that seemed to consume everything. Maybe it wasn't real life, but who needed real life? Our passionate encounters were so much better than real life; in fact being with Stefan felt like a dream come true. And it was happening to me. When it was so intense like that, I felt that for once in my life, everything had come into focus. Everything was clear. I was present, alive, thrilled in the moment.

But sitting there at the table with my parents, I knew what they were going to tell me with their down-to-earth, common sense view of life. They were going to say 'Rachel darling, no matter how good it is, it won't last.' They were going to say that life doesn't work like that, that life can't be that good, that much fun. To them, life was work, responsibility, sacrifice and so on. In their world, you couldn't always get what you wanted. And to them, the bottom line was that whatever I was doing, there was my son to think about.

I knew that was what they were going to say but I didn't want to hear it. Right then, all I wanted was my shot at ecstasy.

We ate for a while in silence. I picked at my food, thinking it was a good thing they didn't know the real truth – that Stefan didn't even want me as much as I wanted him. Ha. I laughed to myself. That was the irony of it. But even if it was only me that was so obsessed, even if it was all a delusion, a dream, I wanted it anyway. I wanted it for as long as it lasted, which I hoped would be for a very long time. That was the truth; my truth. Whatever the cost, I didn't want it to end. I just wanted to keep disappearing down that rabbit hole of bliss and stay there forever.

"So tell us about this Stefan," my mother said, "handsome he must be, but what does he do for a living? Was it Stefan who bought you the fancy clothes?"

"I really don't know exactly what he does, but he works for a man named Albert Giovanni who is the head of a big company called Giovanni International."

"What does this Giovanni International do Rachel?" my father asked.

"As far as I know, they sell heavy machinery all over Europe and the Middle East."

There was a slight lull in the conversation until my mother said, sweetly but firmly, "Look Rachel, why don't you just get on a plane and go back to Amsterdam and have a talk with Jan. Really sweetheart, you owe it to your son."

When I didn't say anything my father added, "At least you can give it a try. Jan might just surprise you and understand. But whatever happens, your mother is right; you owe it to your son. Don't abandon your child for some pleasure that isn't going to last very long. That's what you should be thinking about."

After that, we didn't speak for a while. We were all digesting what had just gone down.

My father wanted to go for a little walk after dinner and I was relieved because I couldn't bear to talk about it anymore. It was a lovely balmy evening and we walked down the Promenade des Anglais. It reminded me of summer vacations when I was a kid.

We felt close together, but also sad that so many of the things we had shared, were past and would never come again. I had this sudden intuition about how it must feel to grow old and see the world you have known and loved fade away. Our lives were passing away so quickly. In a flash we are gone with all our happiness and all our troubles too. It made my own problems seem small and insignificant. The stars were shining down upon us, the same stars that were there when we came into this world and would still be there when we left. What did it matter if I laughed or cried? I was only one more flare in the night, shining brightly for a split second in time. It was the same for my parents. And I had to face it, one day all too soon they too would be passing away. I missed them so much even though they were right there, walking on either side of me. They were my parents, my very own special parents and I would never have any others. They had wedded and bedded and out of that mysterious union, I had emerged with all my hopes and dreams. And they had tried to give me a direction as best they could. Whether they had succeeded or failed didn't really matter at all. We might have quarreled in the past, we might have misunderstood each other at times, but they loved me and I loved them. It was as simple as that.

I stopped and hugged them both, one after the other. They didn't say anything, but I knew they felt the same.

* * *

The next day I put my parents on their plane to Israel.

They left saying, "Now be a good girl Rachel and think about what you are doing! Why don't you just go home to your son?"

It was such reasonable advice. Hearing them talk made everything seem so simple. I was a mother and had a responsibility to my own child. But as soon as I walked out of the airport's glass doors into the sunshine of that splendid Nice morning, I felt that jolt – that marvelous zap of energy running through my body. Wow! And yes, it was that jolt, that zap that sent me on this adventure in the first place. It was such an overpowering sensation and to say it was just a physical thing would have been to underestimate what was going on with me. I was possessed, obsessed, enchained, entranced by an energy I didn't understand. And it didn't have anything to do with the logical, reasonable world my parents lived in and talked about. I had run off in pursuit of something magical. Some might say I just wanted to get my kicks, but whatever it was, the truth was, I wanted more.

Maybe I should go home and maybe I would, but not just yet!

Feeling that jolt of energy course through my body made me remember the day I met Stefan and I shivered with pleasure. It was an early summer day at Zandvoort beach; I was there, enjoying the sun and sea with little Daniel. We'd been there all afternoon and it was early evening – most people were gone or leaving the beach. The sun was sinking slowly in the Western sky. I remembered how cool and peaceful it was and how I was just lounging around enjoying the tranquility and the evening air while Daniel played close by in the sand. All of a sudden this blond Adonis came out of nowhere and asked me if I had a light. I hadn't noticed him before that moment, but apparently he must have been lounging somewhere nearby because he had seen me. (I later found out that he had been sitting moodily on the beach, feeling low because he had just split again from his Dutch wife Monique and their two small daughters – Linda and Sabine. They had been having this on and off relationship for quite a few years until finally Monique had asked for a separation. She was fed up with his uncommunicative ways and the fact that he was away so much on business because of Albert. But obviously at the time, I didn't know any of this.)

A couple of young Indians were making food on a small grill not far from where I was sitting and one of them ran over and asked us if we would like to join them. Daniel jumped up and said "yeah!" because he was hungry and so it all happened so naturally. We laughed and joined the Indians and got to talking as we munched on their lovely food. (The Indians thought we were a couple and laughed heartily when we said we didn't know each other.)

So truly it was as if the gods had arranged our meeting (and of course they had). I found it easy being with him in the cool evening air – and I liked his quiet ways. From the very first moment, I felt as if we were being drawn to each other by this powerful magnetic force and there was nothing we could do about it. I remembered I couldn't take my eyes off this blond Adonis – and he kept looking at me too. We stayed until late in the evening; and by then it was obvious we would meet again.

* * *

When I got back to our hotel suite, Stefan was sitting on the armchair with his feet up on the windowsill. He was talking on the phone. All I could think of was how good he looked, how inviting, how sexy. He had on tight-fitting underwear, which revealed his broad shoulders and muscular arms. He had just taken a shower and his wet blond hair was combed straight back off his face. He looked around at me and motioned me to be quiet.

"Happy Birthday little Linda," he was saying into the phone in a special voice I'd never heard him use before. "How old are you now? Five years old! Did you get the present Daddy sent you?"

My mood of sex and adventure vanished when I realized who he was talking to – his youngest daughter Linda. His wife and two daughters were still living in Amsterdam. And today was the little one's birthday. Funny, but up until that moment I hadn't really thought of Stefan as being a father (though of course I knew he was) or of him being able to speak to a child in that kind of warm, friendly Daddy voice.

I felt vain and stupid hearing him talk to his little daughter like that. Maybe deep down inside, he scorned me because I'd run off with him and left my own son. Maybe he thought I was a pushover, a woman of no character, with only a hot cunt to speak for me. Mentally I began packing my suitcase to catch the next plane back to Amsterdam. My parents said I should go back, Stefan must be thinking the same thing. What was there left for me to do? I really did miss my son.

I went to the bedroom and sat down on the bed while Stefan chatted and laughed with his daughter.

But still, I told myself, this was the first time I'd ever been away from my son and I hadn't been gone very long. Didn't I have a right to a little vacation? But who was I kidding? This wasn't exactly a vacation – this was an uprising – a full-scale rebellion! Looking back, I could honestly say I'd tried; I really had, for years. I'd tried to convince myself that my life with Jan was great. But it just didn't wash. It wasn't enough. I hadn't taken care of me. I hadn't nurtured the woman I was. In fact it had gotten so bad that I no longer even knew who I was. Oh yes, I was a mother and a wife, but it all seemed so tame after the great hopes and dreams of my younger years. Back then I thought I was going somewhere, thought I was going to do something, be someone, and achieve something that mattered. And now all I had was the crushing frustration of a life I had freely chosen with a man who turned out to be a real drag. And I hadn't wanted to admit it, at least not until I met Stefan.

Stefan came to me in the bedroom after he said goodbye to his daughter. I guess I looked depressed because he sat down and put his arm around me and said, "Was seeing your mother and father that bad?"

"Oh no... not really," I mumbled.

"Well then, what is it?"

"It was just... just hearing you talk to Linda like that..."

"Oh come on Rachel, you knew from the beginning that I have two small daughters. They are very dear to me and I am sorry their mother and I are not together to take care of them.

You know that."

"Stefan, do you think I should go back to Amsterdam?"

"You should do whatever you have to do – but not right now!" he said and laughed. "How did we get on this subject anyway?" He pushed me playfully back on the bed. He was determined to make me forget. It wasn't hard to do. He kissed me and I couldn't resist him. There was just something about him, something...

He undressed me expertly and then did what he always did. He took off his underwear and then positioned himself, completely naked, over me with his arms outstretched as if he was about to do push-ups. He surveyed my waiting body and then lowered his firm suntanned body slowly down upon me, touching me gently as I closed my eyes in a swoon. He knew I liked it like that, liked it when he teased me with the touch of his exquisite body until I was wet, wet, wet. And then, when he knew I was ready, he entered me slowly and lay very still on top of me, letting me feel his manhood. And when I sighed that special sigh of intense delight, which he knew so well, he pressed himself deeper into me. I'd never been with a man who fucked like he did. It was always the same – and even if it was missionary through and through, he had a very special talent for it. A very special way of moving slowly in and out of me, which never failed to light my fire. And even though he made the same moves every time, it always worked. Because there was just something about the trancelike way he moved his beautiful body, which always turned me on. Something about the slow, rhythmical movements he made that I loved. And then he'd pick up speed and move slightly faster – and then faster. And I loved it even more. Loved the way his slow deliberation would always lead to that special moment when I felt the thrill of his hard body gaining speed and momentum. Then nothing could deter him. And he would keep his eyes closed and continue to breathe ever so quietly even as his excitement mounted. Then it was all higher, higher, higher and deeper, deeper, deeper – into that pool of intense ecstasy where I could surrender completely – to his rhythm, his guidance, and to the energy that enveloped us. He did not rush, he never did. Nor did he speak as some men do, or alter his rhythm or the flow of it. The strength of his body, and his arm muscles allowed him to flow onward until we met, and found each other, in the passion and power of being together, and coming together.

Aaahhh… the incredible sweetness of him. Of us.

Afterwards my blond Adonis propped himself up on one elbow and looked down at me. His face was open and suddenly vulnerable. He flicked some strands of hair away from my face.

"You know I never met a woman like you before…"

I did not reply but waited, quite sure he was about to say something important, something I desperately wanted to hear, something I thought I'd never hear him say.

"Rachel, I just want you to know," he said softly, slowly, "… that no matter what happens… I really do…"

There was a knock on the door.

We both lay very still. Damn! I hoped whoever it was would go away. Who could it be anyway? No one ever came to our hotel. But the knocking went on.

"Open up Stefan, hurry up! It's important. Come one. It's me, Joey."

The banging continued.

"Merde!" Stefan drew away from me.

"I'm coming Joey, hold on!" he shouted back.

He put on his underwear.

"Rachel, go out to the bathroom and get dressed. I forgot to tell you we're going to a party at Albert's house on Cap Ferrat today. So dress up nice."

I grabbed my robe and rushed to the bathroom, closing the door behind me. Damn.

I pressed myself against the door to hear what was going on. Two men entered the suite. They were speaking French and they were in a hurry. I turned the water on in the sink. I didn't want Stefan to think I was listening. They were talking so fast I didn't understand much, but I did understand when Stefan said, "Joey, no, not again. Not another car bomb!"

The man called Joey replied, "We just got word."

"Merde," said Stefan, "does Albert know about this?"

"Yes, and he's not happy at all. It's making our operations very difficult."

"Merde," I heard Stefan say again.

I didn't dare listen to more.

I wondered what was going on. It sounded serious, dangerous, risky, but I didn't dare ask. Stefan never talked to me about what kind of business they were in (but then again, Stefan never talked to me about anything). And it seemed to be understood that as far as business matters were concerned, I was to be kept completely out of it, whatever it was. Was it chivalry on Stefan's part? Or was it just the man/woman thing in this part of the world? I was curious to know more and knew I should care more, but the truth was I didn't. The truth was I felt like a million. I felt like a fool. I felt enchanted, entranced, insane. I felt wonderful, wild, happy. My life was a mess and my Adonis was about to tell me that he loved me. I was sure; positive! So I wondered – was this it? Was this true love? He was about to say it, I knew it. I knew it. I knew he loved me. And regardless, the lovemaking was divine. I slid down onto the cool tile bathroom floor as the thoughts whirled round and round in my head.

* * *

Albert's house on Cap Ferrat was unbelievable, perched overlooking the Mediterranean. It turned out he wasn't just rich, he was fabulously wealthy. A house like his on Cap Ferrat meant he was very well established indeed.

We walked in through a polished wooden entrance gate onto

a meticulously groomed, Zen style lawn surrounded by swaying palm trees set in round stone beds. An amazing stone terrace sloped and curved down to a swimming pool. Well-dressed men and women were scattered around the pool talking in small groups. Two striking looking women were swimming and laughing in the clear blue pool while several men were standing by, watching them, making jokes and drinking champagne. Discreet white-jacketed waiters moved quietly from group to group with drinks and hors d'oeuvres. I didn't see Albert anywhere. Stefan nodded at several of the people but seemed to be looking for someone special. He led me towards a small group of people sitting on stunningly modern white garden chairs.

"Ah, there is Michelle, I need to talk to her for a minute," Stefan said.

Two men got up and came towards us.

"So this is Rachel," said one.

"Rachel, this is Joey and Carl, they were up at our hotel this afternoon. You missed them, remember?" he smiled. "Carl, entertain Rachel for a few minutes will you? I need to talk to Michelle."

"With pleasure."

Joey was a dark, handsome North African. Carl was tall and thin with a warm smile and gay funny eyes.

Stefan left us for a beautiful French girl with short black hair. He whispered something in her ear and she stood up, took his hand, and they walked away.

Carl grinned, "Don't worry Rachel, Michelle just got back from Beirut. Stefan just wants to talk to her about it."

"What's it all about?" I asked.

"Come, let's go over there," Joey pointed to a cool shady spot under some old trees.

"The first thing you must learn when you join Albert's family," said Carl leaning against one of the trees, "is never ask questions!" He looked at me with impish smiling eyes. Was he serious?

"Oh come on Carl, don't scare her!" Joey broke in. Was he laughing too? "Now tell me, where on earth did Stefan find you?"

"I met Stefan at Zandvoort, a beach just outside in Amsterdam."

"Amsterdam!" they both exclaimed.

"Yes, what's so strange about that?"

"But you can't be Dutch," Joey cried, "you're almost as dark as I am!"

"I'm American."

"Oh… so what were you doing in Amsterdam? Just visiting?"

"Oh no, I've lived there for almost seven years now."

"Seven years? How can you stand it?" cried Joey.

"It's not so bad," I laughed, "my husband is Dutch."

"Your husband?"

"Yes, and Amsterdam is a beautiful city, you know."

"Well," said Joey, "I've never been there so I really don't know. I'm from Algeria but two of my brothers lived and worked in Amsterdam. Both of them married Dutch women but Armand, the younger one, came home quickly."

I had to laugh at the serious expression on Joey's face.

"There's nothing funny about the stories they told," he continued. "What is it with the women up north? Armand's wife wanted to work, you know, and didn't want to have children. What kind of a woman is that? And when he insisted, she left him. He is a hard worker and he just wanted to take care of her so she wouldn't have to work. But she wanted to be independent. Is that the way women are up there?"

"Well yes," I replied smiling, "most women in The Netherlands work."

"But why? What do they want? You think they look so beautiful… all nice and blond, but when they start to talk and you hear what they are thinking… anyway that's what my brother said. And he said they're all like that. My older brother Ali has two children with his Dutch wife and she won't let him take his children to Algeria to visit our old mother because she is afraid he will kidnap his own children and never go back to The Netherlands again. And my old mother is too weak to visit them."

"I'm sorry to hear that but the truth is women are independent in northern Europe and have their own money and can decide things for themselves."

"But is it necessary?" he asked. "I mean if a woman has a good man, why should she want those things? A woman's place is at home. She should be happy to give her husband children. That's how it is where I come from."

How could I tell him we grew up in different worlds?

"Things are different in northern Europe and men and women are brought up in another way. We are taught that men and women are equal and should have equal opportunities to live the life they choose. So men and women act much more alike and they think and work together. And when women are independent, they usually don't have so many children. It's not their only priority anymore. So yes, it's very different." "But how can we have a good life without the difference between men and women? Can you tell me that?"

When I didn't reply, he continued, "And what about you Rachel? Are you like that too?"

"Well I have a son if that's what you mean. And I stayed home and took care of him for quite a while, but I got bored and well here I am... I ran off from my husband too."

Joey looked shocked.

"Why did you leave him? Was this Dutch husband of yours such a bad guy?"

"Oh no, he was an ok guy."

"I'm sure he was," a voice said behind me. I felt hands on my shoulders and I knew from the electric shock running through my body that it was Albert.

"Let's not upset our guests, Joey," Albert said. "When will you learn that the whole world doesn't necessarily think like you and your brothers?" He smiled.

"Pardon," said Joey, and bowed before me.

"Come," Albert said to me, "Let me show you my house."

I looked around for Stefan, but he was nowhere in sight.

* * *

On the way up to Albert's house, we met a big, bear-like man who seemed rather flustered. He spoke to Albert in German, excitedly. Beads of sweat clung to his forehead. Suddenly he stopped in the middle of a sentence and stared at me. His hand moved toward my shoulder.

"Rachel, this is Felix Fischer from Hamburg. I am doing a little business with him. Would you be kind enough to give him your hand? He doesn't speak English but he seems to be quite taken by you."

I shook hands with Mr. Fischer. Then Albert and I walked into the house.

After showing me around the most amazing house, he took me downstairs to his study. It was in the lower corner of the house and because of the slope of the garden; the huge picture windows were above ground looking out over the sea. The view was breathtaking. His long desk faced the windows so he could look out while he worked. I liked that. Further back in the room there was a low couch and I imagined him sleeping there at times.

"Will you drink something?" he motioned towards the couch.

"No thank you. The champagne by the pool on an empty stomach was more than enough for me," I laughed uneasily.

Being suddenly alone with Albert made me tremble all over. I hadn't forgotten the intensity of our first meeting and the wave of liquid desire he had awakened in me. I wanted to act nonchalant and tried to, but couldn't. There was just something about the man that drew me to him; he exuded this strange, magnetic power. He came over to me, standing as I was in the middle of the room, and laid his hands on my bare shoulders. I was sure he felt me trembling. In the background, Music for Zen Meditation by Tony Scott played softly.

"Come my dear, don't be so serious," he said, brushing my hair away from my face, "it's not good for you."

"What do you mean?" I replied, feeling unsure of myself.

"You're wearing yourself out for no good reason."

"Really... I'm not sure I understand."

"Oh yes you do... you are thinking and worrying all the time and it's exhausting you. Always trying to figure things out, trying to deduct what's going on, speculating, worrying. You're probably worrying about your son right now, tormenting yourself because you ran off to have your little fling with Stefan."

"Well what's wrong with that?"

"There's nothing wrong with watching what's going on, but you do more than that. You keep turning things over and over in your mind until you wear yourself out instead of enjoying the present moment. Come and sit down on the couch with me, I want to tell you something."

We sat down.

"Many years ago I spent some years in the Far East and one of the most important things I learned there was that if you want to do anything, enjoy anything, accomplish anything, achieve anything, you have to focus your energy on that one thing and forget everything else that is going on around you. You have to disregard everything else and focus your attention at whatever it is you're going to do – and then do it. I know it sounds very simple, but it's really very difficult to do. Most people don't succeed in life because they scatter their energy too much. Instead of focusing on the task at hand and on the present moment, they waste their energy worrying about what happened yesterday or what's going to happen tomorrow. So they're rarely really present and focused in the moment. And as a result, they don't succeed at what they're trying to do and they don't enjoy the present moment for what it is."

I wondered why he was telling me this. Why me?

He went on.

"In some traditional Eastern disciplines, they teach the idea that you have to divide your mind up into compartments. One compartment for this situation and another compartment for that situation. When you're not actually doing something about a situation or problem, you simply put it in its compartment and forget about it until the appropriate time. Otherwise you are just wasting your energy and exhausting your nervous system. What can you do about your son right now? Nothing, right? So why worry about him? You are just wasting your energy. Save it until you can actually do something about it. Otherwise it's exhausting... what I'm trying to tell you sweet Rachel... is to relax a little... you can just let yourself go... really." He smiled reassuringly.

"Look," he continued, "I have become a very successful businessman. Do you know why?"

"Sure, because you're smart."

"Well it's not just that," he smiled, "It's also because – fortunately for me – I've learned how to focus my attention and my energy. That's the real secret of my success."

"Albert, why are you telling me all this?"

He gazed into space.

"I should have met you before you married and had a son."

"What do they have to do with it, now that I've left them?"

"You'll go back to them and probably soon... but until you do..." he moved closer to me, "let's see what happens..."

He kissed me on the mouth while his hand moved up my leg. Suddenly the door to his office swung open. It was Stefan. He

He did more to me that night, but by then I was so wiped out between the drink, the sex and the revelation that I could do such things that it didn't really penetrate the haze I was in. He was getting more and more uninhibited and rowdy and the last time he put his hands around my neck, which really scared me. But fortunately for me, he was too drunk to do more and fell over sideways on the bed and passed out. I thanked my lucky stars and groped my way to the bathroom. Ugh, I had to get away. I took a long, cold shower, which sort of woke me up. Then I put on my dress and quietly let myself out of the apartment.

* * *

After that I walked. And I walked. It was 4 am. Finally I stopped at a small café and drank two cups of black coffee – that helped. I was still dazed, but also hungry. So I ordered a sandwich and ate, amazed that food could taste so good. Was it just my imagination or what? Or the black coffee after all that went before it? In a strange kind of way, I was euphoric and felt like singing. Was this how an escaped prisoner feels? Or was it just the good pussy bad pussy syndrome? Which one was I? I couldn't decide. All I knew was I felt empty, happy and that nothing mattered. Life was just a dream. So what if I came or went? Was up or down? I'd never get it to work out like I thought it should, no matter how hard I tried. So why try? Why not just give up and go with the flow? It didn't seem to matter all that much anyway.

So I just sat there, staring down into the empty coffee cup, wondering. Wondering – was I still me, after all the things I'd done that evening? I knew I looked the same but I certainly didn't feel the same.

And I also wondered – was this really freedom? The freedom to be and do what I truly wanted… Was it? I wasn't so sure anymore. Maybe this wasn't freedom at all but just a more refined form of the ancient enslavement and subjugation of women by men? Was that what this was? Was it just me, another woman, doing the bidding of the men around me? Was that all it was? All covered up in fancy clothes and money? It sure felt like it. But the truth was no one forced me. I had chosen this subjugation freely. No one held a gun to my head or beat me. I did it because I wanted to. I had chosen freely. And that of course was the basic premise of the whole feminist movement, that women should have the right to choose. And I did... or so I thought. No one forced me to do anything. I agreed to everything – or almost everything. Or did I? My head was spinning. I was a consenting adult wasn't I? Yes that was the bottom line. No one forced me. So did that mean that I was still free even if I had freely chosen submission? Subtle right... and how did my neediness, my need for kicks, the way I was programmed, how our society regards women – how did all that go into the crazy mix of what I had just done that night? And what about my insatiable yearning for ecstasy, my hot pussy...oh me oh my... there she was again, there was good pussy bad pussy raising her mischievous head again. I had to smile to myself... maybe one day I'd figure her out, figure it all out... and find out whether this really was liberation or bondage.

That was when I looked up and saw Albert standing in the open doorway of the empty cafe, gazing at me with his dark, penetrating eyes. I shivered all over. When he realized I'd seen him, he walked slowly over to my table. He didn't smile. "I wanted to see if you were okay," he said.

I thought for a moment.

"Yeah, I guess so," I said, nodding slowly to myself.

"Come," he said, stretching out his hand, "let's get you out of here."

Out of here? I was surprised. Out of here, coming from him? The man who had masterminded what I'd just been through. What, was he regretting what he'd done?

I got up.

He took my arm, as if he was helping a wounded soldier.

He supported me and steered me out to his waiting Porsche.

Once he had me snuggled nicely in, he took off, driving fiercely and silently to his house on Cap Ferrat. We didn't speak.

When we got to the house, he led me in, took me to his bedroom, undressed me and put me to bed. I was asleep before my head hit the pillow.

Some hours later, I woke up and stumbled out to the bathroom. I had to get rid of the taste and smell of Felix, so I brushed my teeth and took a hot shower. Then I went back to bed and fell fast asleep again. When I woke up later it was past noon. Albert came in and tended to me like a sick child, bringing me breakfast in bed. He sat on the edge of the low bed, watching me eat hungrily. We still hadn't spoken.

When I finished eating, he removed the tray and came and sat on the edge of the bed again. He pushed the hair back from my face and looked at me carefully. "I'm sorry about last night," he said ruefully. "It was wrong of me..."

When I heard his words, it was like a dam burst inside me and I broke down crying.

"I should have known," he continued slowly, "I should have respected you for who you are Rachel, from the beginning..." His words only made me sob more. I was so exhausted, confused, and mad. I didn't know what to make of him or of myself or of what I was feeling.

Then I stopped crying and looked at him. "Albert" I said slowly, "I must know...was it liberation or bondage? What happened last night? Which was it... please tell me! I must know!"

When I said those words, he burst out laughing. "Oh Rachel, dearest Rachel! You are simply a miracle. A miracle! Where have you been all my life?" He bent forward and took my face in his hands and hungrily kissed my lips. I was surprised by his hunger. There was something about him, a depth I'd never met before in any man. I remembered how I'd wanted him the last time we were together. How true and real it had seemed at the time. But was it still true now – after all he had put me through?

He drew back from me and sighed. "The wise would say true liberation is only to be found in freedom from the bondage to our desires."

When I didn't reply, he continued. "I studied for years in the East when I was young – with a Zen master. Only to find myself a slave to my own raging desires. And now there is you. Here in my bed." He smiled. "Liberation will just have to wait. A little longer."

He pulled back the covers and put his hands on my naked breasts. I had forgotten I was naked. I sighed at his touch, not knowing if I was mad at him anymore or where life was taking me. So I let him. His caress was gentle and kind. I sank back into the pillows and soon he was kissing my neck and breasts. He sat up again, unbuttoning his shirt.

"Albert, I should call Stefan."

"Don't worry, I sent him to Cairo on business last night." He was pulling off his pants. "I told him I'd look after you." There was just the tiniest of smiles at the corner of his lips as he said these words, while his hands were seeking my breasts again. I didn't even have time to pout because he bent forward to kiss me, whispering, "Now will you turn off that little head of yours and stop worrying! Everything will work out just fine. I promise you..."

Good pussy bad pussy. Liberation bondage... I couldn't know and didn't know. All I knew was the intensity of his hands and his mouth, bearing down on me, like before making me surrender and follow his every move. And even though I was sore after the rough treatment Felix had given me the night before, I felt my hips begin their little dance, quite on their own, as Albert reached down to touch me and caress my wet pussy. He was gentle and I was sure he knew I was sore.

"Hmmm," he sighed moving softly with me and pleasuring me in ways I did not know were possible. And when I was moaning and begging him to take me, he finally entered me, plunging himself ever deeper into my waiting womb. And there it was again, the intense thrill of being possessed by this incredible man. And once again his timing was perfect, his touch exquisite, and we exploded together, into the mystical, beautiful space of his big white bed.

Oh Albert!

* * *

The next day and a half with Albert was absolute magic. It was as if we lingered in a space I'd never inhabited before, a world of slow deliberate colors and tastes and calm. Just like the lawn that surrounded his house where everything was perfect and quiet. There was a tranquillity in the air and in us. And now that there were no people at the house, it all belonged to us. And we filled the empty space with an intensity of beingness that I'd never experienced before. And even though I hardly knew the man, I did know him and knew him well. In fact, I felt I'd always had known him, such was the power of his focus and our coming together that he had made it so. So it was strange and intense and wonderful beyond words – I simply couldn't explain it to myself. I was too overwhelmed. And I was confused too and wondered about Stefan, the man I was supposed to be in love with who was coming back from Cairo soon. What about him? How did he fit into all this? And what about me and my 'real' life back in Amsterdam and my child who I would not abandon? And what about Albert? Did he feel the same intense connection between us as I did... and if he did... what was he going to do about? I just didn't know and couldn't know... and we never got a chance to talk about it because all of a sudden he had a business emergency in Beirut and had to fly off at a moment's notice. And just like that the magic tranquil space we'd shared was gone – puff – evaporated – as quickly as it had begun. But what about the strange, powerful connection between us – was that gone too? Or would it continue… would it stand the test of…

And then I heard him saying like an echo from afar, "I'll call you when I get back."

And off he went and off I went too – back to the hotel in Nice to wait for Stefan's return from Cairo the next day.

* * *

By the time Stefan returned the next day, the world had changed. Significantly.

And not because of Albert.

The world, or I should say, my world shifted on its axis on that particular morning. It was eerie how it happened; I woke up that morning in a cold sweat and knew. Knew something was wrong. The sun was streaming in through the open window, but I knew something was desperately wrong. I was sweating, freezing.

How could I have forgotten? How could I possibly have forgotten?

I was glad Stefan wasn't there. Glad I was alone.

My hands were trembling. I felt hot and cold all over.

I fumbled in my purse looking for my calendar.

But of course you idiot, you're way overdue. You don't need to look at your calendar to figure that out. How long has it been? How long overdue? Why didn't you think of it before? You should have had your period ages ago. Ages ago sweetheart! How could you forget? Was it all this high living? All the sex and men that made you forget? Forget you're a woman. Are you totally blind? Or what?

What were you thinking?

What?

Good pussy bad pussy!

I had this sinking feeling… sinking…

But I knew it was true immediately. I just knew. I was

pregnant.

Pregnant!

Your breasts aren't just sore from all the sex; they're sore because you're pregnant! *Pregnant stupid! Pregnant!*

My mind worked feverishly trying to figure out when it happened.

And then I thought – oh my God, who's the father? Was it Stefan or could it have been my husband? I'd actually slept with Jan right before we left Amsterdam. Idiot! Who...

Pregnant!

It hit me again – like a blow to the stomach... *another baby! Me? No way! What was I going to do? Oh Jesus!*

I grabbed my clothes and rushed out of our suite – and headed straight to the nearest pharmacy. I had to find out right away.

And once I knew, I stayed away the whole day... walking, walking, walking.

Good pussy bad pussy! Fuck.

* * *

When I got back to our suite, Stefan was sitting in the armchair gazing out the huge panorama window, but he got up quickly and came to me. He embraced me. Then he put his hands on my shoulders and looked at me.

"Are you ok?" he asked.

"Me?" I mumbled, looking at the floor. "Yeah I guess so." Then I realized he was referring to that night a few days ago when I'd been with Felix. Yes he was referring to my famous, or was it infamous, night with Felix. I'd almost forgotten about it, it seemed so long ago. Inwardly, I laughed. Yes, it really did seem like ages ago... my night with Felix... and then there had been Albert, passionate, intense Albert for two days and nights afterwards. And then I wondered – did Stefan and Albert always share their women like this? Who did I belong to? Who did I love? Who...

Stefan interrupted my reverie.

"Rachel, tell me what is it... was it that bad?" He pulled me over to the sofa and we sat together. I didn't speak for a long time and he didn't try to force me. Instead he sat quietly with his arm around me, his warmth encircling me. He really did care about me and now he was finally beginning to show me his feelings. I didn't want to break the spell, but I knew I would have to say it, sooner or later. I moved away from him.

"Was it really that bad?" he asked again. "You know I didn't want it to happen! You know that!"

"Yes I know and yes it was bad, but it's not that."

"Then what is it?"

"Stefan," I forced myself to look him in the eye, "I'm pregnant."

"You're what?"

"I'm pregnant."

I felt the door closing.

"Really?"

"Yes, I took a pregnancy test... actually I took two!"

Then he said slowly, very slowly, "It's funny, but I had a feeling you were. When did you find out?"

"Just today, but I've been pregnant for a while."

Pause.

"I must have gotten pregnant just around the time we came to Nice. Either right before we left, or one of the days right after we got here."

Silence.

I had to say it. I had to force myself.

"That means Jan could be the father too," I said slowly.

"What? You slept with him?"

Silence.

"I thought you two were finished."

"I visited him once, right before we left..."

"Oh merde, Rachel!" Stefan threw his towel on the floor and walked back over to the window. He stood looking out for a long while. Then he turned towards me and said, "Rachel, you'll have to get an abortion. Albert knows everyone down here. I'll call him and get him to arrange it."

"I figured you'd say that, but I just don't think I can do it."

"What do you mean?" He looked surprised. "You can't be serious Rachel. What would you do with another baby?"

"I don't know... I just don't know..."

* * *

After that, Stefan and I didn't talk about it anymore. He didn't want the baby. He wouldn't take me before with one child, he had made that clear. So now there was no way he was going to take me with another child on the way. And I wouldn't have an abortion that much I knew. It wasn't that I was against free abortion; it was just that I didn't think it was something to be used like a convenience store when women got into trouble. Fucking around had consequences and now in my case the consequence was that I was pregnant. That was just the way of it. And I believed in the sacredness of the new life I was carrying... and I also believed that unless I was critically ill or in eminent danger, it was my sacred duty to protect and nurture this new life as best I could. So there really wasn't much to say or talk about, was there? But that didn't change the fact that I was raging mad at Stefan – and disappointed. Raging mad and disappointed that he was abandoning me like that. Raging mad and disappointed that he didn't want me just because I was pregnant. In my head I shouted to the heavens... *Here is the man I'm supposed to be crazy about, here's the man I'm supposed to be head over heels in love with, and now he's abandoning me because I am carrying a child which is probably his.* I just couldn't get my head around it.

I felt like weeping, I felt like screaming. But I couldn't and didn't because in fact I was paralyzed, frozen by a horrible sense of doom. I simply didn't know what to do.

And what could I do?

No matter how I looked at it, I always came up with the same answer – nothing, absolutely nothing.

I couldn't change Stefan. That was obvious. For some reason losing his first family had been so traumatic for him, had caused him so much pain that he felt he couldn't deal with more. What the backstory was, I would never know because he never told me. Not the details anyway. But I did know that according to him, he couldn't deal with having another family. He'd told me that from the very beginning. Yes, he'd said it up front. He'd told me not to expect anything, he told me that even though he wanted me, he didn't want me with the child I already had. It was me alone, or nothing. He made that clear. From day one. So even though he was the probable father of the child I was now carrying, there was absolutely nothing I could do about it. He had already laid it all out.

And talking about it was out of the question. You simply couldn't talk to Stefan, it wasn't an option. He wasn't like that, had never been. If you tried, he'd just gaze at you with those clear blue eyes of his or he'd laugh and push you into bed...

Sometimes I wondered how many women he had gazed at like that... or pushed into bed like that...

So I was at a loss, in shock. Grieving, all messed up. And it was all pent up inside of me together with this baby.

And then there was Albert!

Albert!

What about him? What about the passion he'd awoken in me? What about the powerful connection between us?

I hadn't heard from him and wondered if he was back from Beirut. The very next day the phone rang and I knew it was Albert before Stefan handed me the phone.

"Rachel, come downstairs, I want to talk to you." Just hearing his voice made my heart flutter. *Oh Albert!*

"OK," I said and gave the phone back to Stefan.

"Albert wants to talk to me Stefan. Did you tell him I was pregnant?"

"Yes."

Albert was waiting for me in the lobby.

The first thing he did when he saw me was brush my hair from my face. Then he lifted my face towards his and gazed at me with those dark, penetrating eyes of his. He didn't say a word but took my arm and led me out of the hotel to his waiting Porsche.

He roared off and drove to a secluded spot along the coast and pulled over.

The sky was incredibly blue that day.

Albert pulled me to him and kissed me passionately on the mouth. And I knew in that moment that I loved him. I was that sure.

"Rachel darling, you can't be serious about not having an abortion."

"So Stefan told you I was pregnant."

"Yes, he did."

There was a long silence.

Then I took Albert's hand and said very slowly, "But I am serious."

"But what will you do with a baby? There's no future for you here with a baby, you must see that."

"Yes, I do." I thought I was going to cry at the injustice of it, but I didn't.

"But Rachel," he said and sighed, "*We* were doing so nicely… *we* were…."

When I didn't reply he continued, "I'm not ready to lose you so quickly, not yet. Won't you at least think about it? Please!"

"But I already have thought about it Albert… I've thought

about it a lot. And it's really very simple. Very, very simple! Can't you see… it's the sacredness of life we're talking about… the sacredness of life."

There was a very long silence. I could feel the beating of my heart. Then he cleared his throat as if he had a lump in it and said ever so slowly, "…but of course you are right my dear darling Rachel. But of course… it *is* the sacredness of life we're talking about…"

The sky was so very blue that day, so very blue. I felt the pressure of tears gathering behind my eyes, but none came out.

Then he said, as if suddenly waking from a dream, "Rachel, come and stay with me at my house… please!"

Oh how I wished I could… oh how I wished. But I knew I couldn't.

The sky was still so very blue.

And then I said something that surprised even me, "You were right Albert. You were right all along. I have to go back to my son in Amsterdam."

When he heard those words, he turned on the engine and roared back to the hotel.

He didn't say another word but there was real pain in his eyes when I kissed him goodbye and got out of the car.

* * *

Two days later, I left the Riviera. I still remember how Stefan looked that morning as he closed the door on his way out to meet Albert. See you later. We couldn't say goodbye. But he knew. And I looked at him, really looked at him, the way you look at someone when you know you're not going to see them again for a long, long time or maybe ever again… I made a mental picture of him to take with me. One I would be able to take out in the years to come and enjoy. In the dark of night when I was all alone and wanted to feel his presence. He looked so good, so beautiful, so swift, so graceful, so calm. His body an instrument of such fantastic fluidity and grace. Yes I could see why I had loved him so. He was like a classical statue, a true Adonis, his lines so clear, so pure. He moved so lightly on his feet, without a sound, but sure, swift, determined. And his hair fell flat across his forehead as he turned towards me one last time in the doorway.

"See you soon," he said and it pierced my heart.

Goodbye Stefan.

Then I packed my suitcase and left. I took the first flight I could get to Amsterdam.

PART II

AMSTERDAM

I was back in Amsterdam that very afternoon; my adventure on the French Riviera over. My time with Stefan and Albert over! Modern technology moved me faster than my heart could adjust. I felt stunned.

It was October and the colors were different than on the French Riviera. I took a cab to our apartment in downtown Amsterdam. Maybe Jan would be there, though I doubted it. I looked at my watch. It was 4 o'clock. No he'd probably be at our shop. Just the thought that he might be in the apartment got my adrenaline working. How would it be? What would he say? What should I say?

My heart was pounding in my chest as I went up the stairs. I wasn't sure I wanted to see Jan and was afraid he'd be there. I turned the key. The place was empty. I sighed with relief. I walked around the apartment; it looked much smaller than I remembered when it was full of life. It didn't look like Jan was living there either. Everything was neat and tidy. No unmade beds or unwashed dishes, and Daniel's room was exactly as I had left it – with all his toys put away. I was sad my son wasn't there. It was just an empty space without him. I opened the windows and unpacked my clothes. I went out to the kitchen to see if there was any food. Then I called Jan's parents and told them I'd come by and pick up Daniel.

On my way out of the apartment I ran into my neighbor, Ginger. She was my good friend and I was happy to see her. She was older than me, tough and wise. She had a daughter with a black American, but they didn't live together anymore.

"Rachel!" she cried when she saw me. "I didn't know you were back!"

"I just got back an hour ago." We hugged.

"Did you have a good time? I can't believe how great you look."

"Listen Ginger, I've got to run... I'm on my way to pick up Daniel. Can we talk later?"

"Sure, why don't you come over tonight after you put Daniel to bed... then you can tell me everything."

"Super," I said, running down the stairs, but then I stopped and called back, "Ginger... have you seen Jan? It doesn't look like he's been living in the apartment."

"Yeah, I've seen him once or twice."

"Is he ok?" When she didn't answer, I climbed back up the stairs.

"What is it?"

"Well..." she hesitated as if she wasn't sure what to say.

"What? Come on Ginger, tell me."

"Well I ran into him on the stairs the other night with a woman – a real looker. I don't know who she is."

"OK Ginger, well I've got to run, we'll talk tonight." I ran down the stairs.

* * *

Daniel was sitting at the kitchen table, eating cookies and drinking milk and chattering away, telling me his stories about all the things he did while he was at his grandparents. My heart contracted hearing him talk. How could I have ever gone away from him? What was I thinking? I loved him so.

The windows were open and the soft sounds from the street below drifted up. Suddenly it did feel like home again. Then Daniel asked, "Mommy, when is Daddy coming home?"

"Oh soon, sweetie. Soon." I said.

And when he was exhausted from so much talking, I put him to bed, his room already the usual jumble of toys and books. He looked so sweet and innocent as he lay there, trusting the world would be good to him.

When he was fast asleep, I left the door to our apartment ajar and went next door to see Ginger. Her real name was Annemarie, but there was no denying she was one spicy lady. Her apartment was like her life, half Dutch provincial (which she came from) and half super trendy very today and very international. I had always admired the way she could combine so many influences and make such a wonderful home for her daughter and her friends.

"Rachel, if you were having such a good time, why did you leave Stefan and come home all of a sudden? I don't get it."

When I didn't reply she said, "Did you fall out of love or what?"

"No, I still love him."

"Well then what? It doesn't make sense. And you look so terrific."

And when I still didn't reply, she said, "Oh come on sweetie, what's up?"

"I'm pregnant."

"You're what?" She nearly dropped her wine glass she was so surprised.

"I'm pregnant."

"You've got to be kidding, Rachel."

"No, it's true."

"But Rachel, this is ridiculous. What difference does it make if you love the guy?"

"Well actually a lot, especially since I've already got a son that Stefan doesn't want to begin with. Did you know he's got two kids of his own?"

"No really? You never told me that."

"Well he does – and he doesn't want another kid. No way in hell."

"Oh come on Rachel, haven't you heard of abortions? Everybody has them. Even me, I've had two. They're not so bad."

"Maybe not, but I don't want to have an abortion," I said slowly, "It's a life we're talking about... a life in me."

"Come on girl, a woman's got to do what a woman's got to do. I mean what are you going to do with another kid?"

"That's a good question – a very good question." I sighed.

"Abortion the only sensible thing you can do," Ginger shot back, "no matter how nasty you think it is. I mean what are you going to do sweetheart?"

"I really don't know, but I just don't think I could have an abortion. I really don't. It's the sacredness of life we're talking about..."

"But look at your life Rachel? What will you do now? Live alone with two small kids. I mean come on. What a situation. How will you manage? Rachel, it's crazy – just crazy."

"Maybe Jan will take me back."

"Jan? Why would you want him back? After all you two have been through?"

When I didn't answer, she continued, "And what makes you think he'd take another man's child anyway?"

"Ginger, I'm not even sure who the father is. It could be Jan's baby too."

Ginger was quiet, digesting this new piece of information.

"Well who knows, if he thinks it's his baby... oh shit...I really don't know. But why would you want him back?"

It was a good question.

She was quiet again for another minute or two and then continued, "That woman I saw him with... well he didn't look that unhappy to me."

"Yeah, he might not want to come back even if I asked him to. I've thought of that."

"It was obvious you and Jan were having a rotten time this past year. I could see it on your faces. He must have been a drag to live with. You know I always thought he was so uptight. But it takes two to make a mess Rachel, you know that. So somewhere in all this, the truth is, you were itching to get out. Itching to have some good sex and the time of your life. And then when that dream hunk Stefan turned up, well," she laughed, "I would have done the same!"

It was good to have a friend like Ginger, she really understood.

I let out a long sigh, thinking of Stefan. Missing him. And then I thought, *the bum, why didn't he want me more?*

Fortunately Ginger rambled on. "You know the other thing I've been thinking," she said as she poured herself some more wine, "is that it was probably good for Jan that you left him. I mean maybe it helped him get his act together. Who knows? All I know was he sure needed to!"

I laughed. "Yeah, we can always hope!"

"Could be. You never know with men. When I was over at your shop the other day buying some smoothies, I thought Jan looked so much better and the juice bar was so packed with people he didn't even notice me. But I saw him and he, well, just looked, I don't know… a whole lot better. So who knows? Maybe you're cutting out on him like you did was a good thing. Maybe it was a wake-up call for him… You know it's never a good thing to take anything or anyone for granted and he sure as hell took you for granted."

When I didn't reply, she took my hand and squeezed it hard. "But either way Rachel, please think about having an abortion. It seems crazy to me you having another baby!"

* * *

I went to our shop the next day to see Jan. Conflicting emotions rushed through me as I crossed the threshold, but there was no sense in putting it off. Was it love or hate? Or both? My heart pounded in my chest. Just the thought of Jan made me feel like I couldn't breathe. Going back to him would be like getting into a very small box again after Stefan and Albert. *Oh Stefan and Albert – now they were real men, especially Albert.* No sense in denying I had a soft spot for men of the world like them.

The shop, which was a combination juice bar/health food shop, was busy. I couldn't see Jan anywhere. Anton, our partner, said he was in the back, in the office. I went out back to find him. He wasn't pleased to see me and showed it.

"What is it now, Rachel?" was all he said. The iceman cometh.

I just stood there. I couldn't remember what I'd seen in him.

Finally I spoke, "Can we talk Jan, please?"

"What's there to talk about?" He shuffled some papers on his desk.

"Let's go for a walk."

"A walk?"

"Yeah, I have something to tell you."

He sighed deeply like I was such a pain, but after much show of disapproval, he decided to go with me. We wandered around a bit and ended up on a bench under a big tree by one of the canals.

"Well you wanted to talk?" he said, still cold as ice.

There was no putting it off any longer.

"Jan, I'm pregnant."

"You're what?" He looked startled. At least I seemed to have gotten his attention.

"I'm pregnant." I started to cry.

Jan didn't move.

"Who's the father?"

I cried some more and blew my nose.

"Who, I said." He was like an angry schoolteacher scolding a wayward pupil.

"I don't know."

"What do you mean, you don't know."

"I mean I don't know. It could be you or it could be Stefan."

There was a long silence.

And then I said it, said what I was fearing I would say, "Jan, I think you should come home and we should give it another try."

He didn't move or say anything so I rushed on. "Please... I don't want to have an abortion. I simply can't do it. I can't kill this child. So I thought well maybe you'd give us another chance? Couldn't we try just one more time? Couldn't we...?"

Suddenly he was looking at me with this funny little smile on his lips. It was almost cruel. He had this hardness about him, this coldness. I wasn't sure if I loved him at all. No in fact I was sure at that moment that I didn't love him. I was sure I hated him, hated everything about him. But I didn't know what else to do. I was floundering. Alone with one child and now pregnant with another. What was I supposed to do? I felt lost. Maybe I should have called my parents and asked them for help but I was afraid of what they would think about me being pregnant again – and not even knowing who the father was. I wondered if this was why so many women ended up eating humble pie, even in this modern day and age? Was it because we really don't know how to take care of ourselves when the shit hits the fan?

I shivered.

Maybe it was me I hated the most. For getting myself in such a mess. For being so stupid... for...

He sighed and put his arm around me. Feeling him touch me gave me chills. Then he said, "OK Rachel, I'll come home."

I didn't know who I hated more, him or me.

* * *

By the time he came home the next day, I had cleaned up the apartment and made everything nice. He came into the flat just like he always did. Daniel was sitting on the floor, watching TV and I was out in the kitchen when I heard his keys rattle in the door. My heart contracted. What was I doing? Thinking? I had that feeling again, like I couldn't breathe, like I was getting squeezed into a very small box. Daniel hugged him and followed him as he wandered around the apartment, a bit like a stranger.

I knew in my gut it would never work.

I set the table and served dinner. We tried to act normal but everything was different. Daniel was happy we were both home and the family was together again, and it was a blessing to have him to distract us. After we did the dishes and put Daniel to bed, Jan said, "Come Rachel, let's go to bed." I felt the prison gates closing.

* * *

The next day was Saturday and Jan said, "Rachel, I have to go see Jeanette. Get Daniel dressed and we'll go out there together. I want you to come along."

So it was Jeanette Ginger had seen him with.

"Wouldn't you rather go alone?" I asked. "I'll only be in the way." I was still in bed, under the down duvet.

"No, I want you to go with me. It's not like you think. We're only friends; she was really there for me when I was lonely." He started to stroke my hair. I didn't want him to touch me. Fortunately he hadn't wanted to have sex the night before – but I knew I couldn't avoid it for long. It was hard to contemplate after Stefan and Albert. My heart ached; I missed them both so much.

I sat up. "OK Jan, if that's what you want." I got out of bed. Jeanette was the wife of one of Jan's oldest friends. She and her husband Dirk were heroin addicts, and had been for as long as anyone could remember. But surprisingly enough, they had two kids and lived a very straight life – except of course for the fact that he did drug deals from time to time. Dirk was not in the country at the moment, he was away on business, whatever that meant. But it was Jeanette that always had fascinated me because I imagined that every man in the world must be dreaming of having a woman like Jeanette. There was just something about her, something soft and mysterious. I didn't know if it was the heroin that did it, but she had this dreamy quality and always seemed so far away like and quiet. It made her seem infinitely attractive or so I thought.

We parked outside Jeanette's house. They lived in an ordinary house on an ordinary street. Her kids were playing in front of the house but Jeanette was nowhere in sight. Jan greeted her children and they were happy to see him. He pulled Daniel out of the car and he ran over to play with her kids. Obviously Daniel had been there before. Then Jan went up to the open front door of the house and knocked on the doorframe.

"Anybody home?" he called.

Jeanette came rushing out and before she saw me, I saw the look in her eyes when she saw Jan.

"Oh Jan..." she said, and then she saw me and added, "and Rachel."

Maybe Jan thought she was only a friend, but I could see she was in love with him. Even if she did have her own husband and it didn't fit what she said, yes, I could see she wanted Jan. And why shouldn't she? I couldn't blame her for that. After all, I hadn't been there and he needed comfort and she gave it to him. Why shouldn't she have hoped for more?

After we talked about my suntan and vacation for a while I said I would take the kids over to the playground down the street for a while. I knew she wanted to talk to Jan alone.

* * *

When the kids and I got back to the house, we found them sitting under a gnarled tree in the corner of the garden. The leaves were turning and there was a golden light over them. It was so peaceful and I thought Jeanette was quite a woman, heroin or not. There was such an air of quiet around her. Maybe that was why Jan liked to be with her. Or was it because she never contradicted him but always looked at him with such adoration? The reality was she was the exact opposite of me! My blood was hot and I was always searching for that kick, that something special – whatever it was. Jan complained that I was always causing trouble, but what was wrong with wanting more out of life? That was when I realized that life with Jan would never be enough for me and that I probably wouldn't spend five MORE minutes with the man if it weren't because of Daniel – and the child growing in my stomach.

Oh what a mess I'd gotten myself into!

I bit my lip and tried not to think about it.

I approached them and Jan and Jeanette smiled at me, a warm friendly smile and I found myself sitting down and smiling too. The kids played happily and I just sat. I didn't know what to say, so I didn't say anything.

When Jeanette got up to fetch some more tea Jan said, "It's always so peaceful here."

"Yes," I replied, "I can see why you like it here."

* * *

After that, Jan and I drifted cautiously back into the routine of daily life. I wasn't particularly happy or unhappy. I was just doing what I felt I had to do and who knows, maybe Jan felt the same. We didn't talk about it and Jan never mentioned the baby. In fact he never mentioned anything, so I didn't either.

Sometimes I had to admit, I found myself thinking about how would it be to be with a truly powerful man like Albert, someone who was strong and dynamic and could dominate me and fuck me divinely. Strange how Albert sometimes popped up in my reveries; with his dark penetrating eyes and his sensuous, aristocratic lips. For some reason, from the very first moment I saw him, I knew he knew me, saw me, knew my soul. And I found it terribly unsettling and attractive. Oh Albert! But he, like Stefan, was fast becoming nothing more than a figment of my imagination, a memory, a dream. Something I'd buried away when I decided to ask Jan to come back. Jan, my husband, who seemed so… so dull and ordinary in comparison to wise, worldly Albert.

So I guess I was just kidding myself, kidding myself that there might be a chance that my life with Jan could work if I'd really wanted it to. I guess underneath I knew all along it was just a big lie. Because the truth was, I was a volcano of dreams and desires just waiting to erupt. It was just a matter of time.

Then one unusually warm October morning, when Jan was at the shop and Daniel was at kindergarten, I had the urge to go to the beach and see the sea again. The day was so warm and sunny it was nearly like summer so I thought if I was lucky I might even be able to go for a swim. I headed out to Zandvoort just west of Amsterdam. It was nearly deserted when I got there. Only a few stray people sunbathing here and there.

I took off my t-shirt and jeans. I had my bikini on underneath. I lay down on the sand just by the water's edge. The sun was so warm that it didn't really feel like autumn at all so I just lay back and enjoyed the warmth, the sun and the sound of the sea.

I couldn't help but think about Jan and me. What was I doing? It seemed crazy when I thought about it. What future could we possibly have together? But being pregnant had somehow thrown a monkey wrench into the whole thing. I just didn't know what to do and the baby was making me put everything on hold.

I guess I was waiting for a sign.

Then I thought of Stefan and tingled all over at the thought of his sexy body. God I missed him. I wished I could call him, talk to him, hear his voice, feel his divine presence just one more time. Oh Stefan… but the man didn't want me, had made it clear he didn't want me pregnant… had…

Suddenly I became aware of a man besides me, gazing at me. I sat up in a hurry.

"Jesus, you are beautiful," he said.

I couldn't help but smile. Maybe that was a mistake, but thinking about Stefan made me remember my sex. The truth was I was already so bored again with my life with Jan. I just didn't know what to do about it.

He was standing directly in line with the sun, so I couldn't see him clearly, but there was no mistaking the outline of his broad shoulders. He looked good. Strong body, hard muscles, tight-fitting bathing suit. He sat down and I saw his face was slightly pock-marked, but he had a good, strong jaw, straight black hair with a few streaks of grey. Strong hands. Nice. Shit, I thought to myself. I was doing absolutely nothing to attract this, absolutely nothing. I didn't want it or need it, but now that it was here…

"Look," he said, "my name is Frank. You want to go for a swim."

"OK," I said thinking a swim couldn't hurt, "My name is Rachel."

We got up.

"One condition babe," he said with a wicked grin on his face.

"What's that?"

"We swim naked."

"Naked!" He was too much.

"What, don't you dare?"

"Sure I dare," I smiled, knowing he'd trapped me.

He was already out of his bathing suit, running into the water. I took off my bikini and ran after him. I plunged in, head first. The water was icy cold. God it was great to be alive and swim naked in the cold North Sea. Water was a blessed purification that washed me clean. No problem could cling to me now I thought.

I looked for my new friend and saw him swimming towards me with strong confident strokes. I swam swiftly north, parallel to the beach and when I stopped, out of breath, I felt Frank come up from behind and slide his arm around my waist. I squirmed to free myself but he held me tightly. I turned and faced him, trying to pull free, but he was too strong for me.

"Oh come on," I said, but he was already pressing me tightly to his chest and as I lifted my face up towards his, I met his cold sensual lips closing hotly over mine. Such passion in such cold water? He must have read my thoughts because he said, "Damn, I didn't know I could get such a hard-on in such cold water."

I felt him hard and stiff against me. And then a wave from a passing yacht made us stumble a bit and I instinctively put my legs around his waist to keep my balance. I felt him try to enter me, but the water was too cold.

"Let's get out of here," he said, letting me go and taking my hand, pulling me towards the shore. We were both shivering with cold as we splashed back to the beach. Once up on land, he started running towards the dunes, dragging me after him. I ran with him, laughing, sharing his need. On the way, he scooped up my big beach towel so we'd have something to cover ourselves with. And then we were in a little hollow behind the dunes, hidden from view, rolling hungrily on the sandy ground.

"You make me so horny babe, I can't believe it," he was saying as he held me in an iron grip. And I had to admit; he had the same effect on me. I loved the feel of his powerful arms winding tightly around my waist, pulling me to him. I went limp and dug my fingernails into his shoulders. Then I turned my mouth to welcome his hungry lips, feeling myself open and relax even more as he found my depths. And even though it was all happening too fast, I didn't really care. We were a perfect match, in a perfect moment so I just went with it. And in that lovely flow, I felt him swelling inside me, making me feel wobbly and wonderful in a way I hadn't felt since I'd left Nice. Aahh Jan could never fuck me like that.... And then he came, hard and fast, and all too quickly and so did I, hard and fast, and all too quickly, clinging to him.

He was so good – really good – and so was I.

In another time and place, we would have been perfect.

I sighed and looked into his grey flecked eyes keeping him inside me for as long as I could. He understood and we both smiled.

And then we just lay there on my big beach towel, totally content in the warm sun, dozing, dozing.

When I woke up a little later, he was still sleeping. His black grey hair tangled on his forehead. I liked him, but it wasn't the right time for me and there was nothing I could do about it. So I left him lying on my big towel, went back to the beach, picked up my clothes and went home feeling elated and high and slightly awed by what I'd just done. I also knew in my heart of hearts, it was a sign that my relationship with Jan would never work.

Just as I got home, Jan called.

"Where the hell have you been? I've been trying to get you all day. Why didn't you answer your phone?"

My heart sank. "Gee, I guess I didn't hear it…. I was at the beach. I just felt like going for a swim. Is anything wrong?"

"Yeah… your mother called from New York, your father's had a heart attack."

I sat down on the nearest chair.

"Oh Jan… is it…"

"Yeah, it sounds bad."

"I'll call her right away."

"She said she wants you to fly to New York right this minute. She thinks maybe you can see him before it's too late."

PART III

NEW YORK

By the time I got to New York, I was truly spaced out – hoping against hope that my beloved father was still alive. The sudden news of his heart attack – on top of being pregnant, missing Stefan and Albert, and trying to make a go of life with Jan again – was almost more than I could bear. So it was no wonder I hardly recognized my matronly, older sister Marlene standing there at the airport waiting for me. But she recognized me immediately and waved. I walked unsteadily over to her.

"How's Dad?" I asked, but looking at her face, I already knew.

"I'm sorry Rachel, but your father passed away." He wasn't Marlene's father though he always treated her like his own daughter. It made me sad that she called him 'my' father.

"Dead?"

"Yes, he passed away a few hours ago. He never regained consciousness and maybe it was just as well…"

I stood there, stunned.

"How's mother?" I stammered.

"Oh you know mother… she really loved Jerry, but she knew he was getting on…" She sighed. "But some things are impossible to prepare for."

I felt as if I'd been turned to stone. A river of tears was streaming down my cheeks, but Marlene babbled on unperturbed. "Mother and Jerry were so different… I always thought my father, Morgan, suited her much better. But you never met him did you?"

I just stared at her blankly. What was the woman talking about? My father was dead… had just died… was…! For some reason I noticed that she was wearing far too much jewelry for the time of day and her lipstick was way too red. I felt nauseous, sick. Was this woman really my half-sister? Did we really have the same mother, the same elegant Isabel? Then the thought of my beloved father being dead washed over me again and I cried even more. Everything seemed so dumb and confusing and I was so very tired.

"Come on Rachel, let's go. You'll feel better when we get back to the house," Marlene said, finally noticing I wasn't doing so well. She took me by the arm and led me back to her car, which was very shiny and expensive just like her. I slumped into the seat and watched America fly by. Was my father really dead? Dead!

I was infinitely comforted when I reached my mother's house. I had flown all the way across the ocean to comfort and support her, but she, as usual, was comforting me. How did I have the good fortune to have such a mother? She was not only proud and beautiful, she was a true aristocrat. Even death could not shake her dignity. It was her very core, her essence. I felt so very faded in her presence; her strength and character once again amazed me.

"Oh Mother, I'm so sorry," I wept in her arms like a baby.

"So, so Rachel," she said and wept too. "You knew he was getting old. Remember darling he had a good life and was happy to the end of his days."

"I know," I said crying, "but I just can't believe it. It doesn't feel like he's gone, it feels like he's still here."

"But of course my dear, isn't that how it should be?"

"I prayed… so hard…"

"So did I," my mother said, sighing. And then we just sat there in silence for a long, long while, crying. Finally she turned and looked at me, immediately knowing something was up. She wiped away her tears and said, "Now tell me what is happening with you Rachel. Something's going on, I can feel it."

I was happy my sister had left and I was alone with my mother.

"Oh Mom, I've made such a mess of things…" I replied and

cried some more. "But Jan moved back… you know that."

"Yes, when you called I thought it was probably a good idea for you to give it another try. But now, looking at you, I'm not so sure. What's going on?" She held me at arms length. "What's wrong?"

"Mother, I don't want you telling anyone yet, ok?"

"Telling anybody, don't be silly Rachel, I am your mother."

"Not even Marlene. Ok?"

"Telling anybody what my dear? I don't know what you're talking about." She looked very tired and the tears were swelling up in her eyes again.

"I'm pregnant again."

She didn't say anything for a while as the tears streamed down her checks.

"Your father would have been so very, very happy."

That made me cry some more.

Then I laughed.

"What do you think Daddy would have said if he knew that I wasn't sure who the father of the baby is?"

And suddenly it all seemed so ridiculous. Here was death, here was life. My mother saw it too because suddenly she laughed heartily, really heartily, in a way she seldom did, at least not in the presence of others. "Oh my darling Rachel, you are a marvel! Truly! You know," she said wiping her tears away, "I don't believe it would have made a bit of difference to Jerry! Why none at all!"

"Oh momma!" I hugged her with all my might.

"Come now, you go in and sleep for a while. You'll feel better after you've had a nap."

* * *

I woke up several hours later in my father's study. Originally it had been my bedroom, but when I left home, my parents turned it into a study. The room was just right for him and it looked and smelled just like him. I thought it was very kind of my mother to put me in that room. It was her way of letting me be alone with him again. All by myself, just one last time. I put on my jeans and sat down in my father's chair by his desk. Everything was just as if he'd gone for a short walk. His newspapers. An unfinished letter. A faded picture of Isabel and me.

I turned and faced the windows. Outside were the beech trees he loved so dearly.

There was a soft knock on the door.

My mother came and for the first time I could really see how old she was. She looked really terrible and worn out.

"What time is it?" I asked her. It was dark outside.

"About nine," she said. "I think you slept a couple of hours. Are you feeling better now?" She sat down on the crumpled bed.

"I guess so. I just feel so strange… with the jet lag and being pregnant and now with Daddy…"

"I know," she said and sighed. "There are things in life which nothing can prepare you for. You just have to live through them as best you can."

I wandered around the room, touching little things I remembered from my childhood. My mother was lost in some memory so I didn't disturb her. I was trying to reorient myself to the new reality that was unfolding. It wasn't easy.

"Rachel," my mother came back from her reverie and said, "before all the ceremony starts, I wanted to give you this." She took out a small box wrapped in plain brown wrapping paper.

"What is it?" I looked at the box in surprise.

"I really don't know," she said. "Your father just asked me to send it to you a few days ago. He didn't tell me what it was. But he had a strange look in his eyes when he gave it to me. I think he said something like – 'better do it before I get too old and anyway she could probably use it now'. But I didn't know what he was talking about."

I took the little box from her outstretched hand.

"Look, I'll go and make you some dinner dear. You must be absolutely starved. You come and eat when you have opened your package." She smiled sweetly and shut the door firmly behind her. I marveled at her tact. She always knew what was best in every situation. And now she knew that I would want to be alone with my father's gift in that room, which had been both his and mine. Alone with his spirit just a little while longer.

I sat down and took a deep breath, lingering for a while in fond memories of my father. Then I opened the old, worn little box. Inside I found a tightly folded piece of paper, which I lifted up and put aside because underneath I found – to my great surprise – a beautiful little ring. I picked it up. The ring was very small and gold and the small golden band widened out just enough on one side to hold three small diamonds! It was lovely. I put the ring on my little finger. It fit perfectly! Had he known it would fit or was it just a coincidence? I gazed at my little finger in wonder. The old-fashioned ring was so delicate and had tiny carvings around the three small stones. Whose ring had it been and why had my father given it to me? I picked up the tightly folded piece of paper that had been in the box.

I spread the paper out before me on the desk. My father had written the following in very small print: *"My dearest Rachel, This beautiful ring was my mother's. She told me this story when she gave me the ring just before she died. 'When I was a young woman, your father and I were invited to a ball in the City to honor some guests from the old country. I wore the finest gown your father could afford. It was a lovely affair and I admired all the rich and beautiful people, especially the cultivated ladies and gentlemen from Europe. To my great surprise, a famous count asked me to dance. I was both flattered and embarrassed but also relieved when I saw your father was deep in a business conversation at the other end of the ballroom. This count said I was so beautiful that he wanted to run away with me that very moment. When I told him I was married he looked very sad, but he smiled gallantly and said that he would run away with me anyway, if I would. Of course he knew I wouldn't. When the ball was over, I saw him looking at me as I left with your father. I was flattered by his attention but didn't think too much about it because I was sure that such a handsome count flirted with women all the time. So you can imagine how surprised I was when this small box was delivered by a private messenger boy some days later. I was sure he sent it like that so it would come when my husband was not home. Yes it was this very box, with this very ring with the three small diamonds. He wrote a note to me which said, "I cannot forget your beauty. Please accept this ring as a token of my admiration. My mother gave it to me and told me to bestow it upon a beautiful woman who needed confidence. Thus I give it to you so that you will have the confidence that your beauty will never fail you and so that you will have the confidence to use this power wisely." And sure enough, until this day, whenever I felt tired or afraid or unsure of myself, I would take out the ring and gaze at it. I never dared to wear it or show it to your father. But now that I am nearing the end, I want to give it to you, my son, and I ask only that you give it to a beautiful woman who needs confidence. Because this is the confidence ring, as I always called it.' So now you see my dear Rachel why this ring is so special. I never gave it to your mother because, well you know her, does she need it? No I think not. I always thought she was the most poised and confident woman on this earth. But you my darling daughter, you who are both beautiful and a little crazy, I know in your heart of hearts there are lurking vague and dangerous doubts. This you must overcome in yourself. This I wish for you. And so I give you this little ring, to give you the confidence to be yourself, to blossom forth and radiate in this world. Life is very short my dear and it would be terrible to suddenly realize that now one is old and that the inner power or beauty or whatever it was... was never used, had never shone forth. Do not waste yourself or time. Have confidence in yourself in whatever you do and do it fully, with your whole heart. Remember you are a marvelous girl. I love you. Your Father."*

The tears were streaming down my cheeks as I read his letter. Such a good man and such a wonderful father. He knew I needed love and encouragement more than anything else in the world. So I wept for joy at having such a father, a father who loved me so much, and for the sadness of his passing. I would never see his dear, beloved face again.

When I had composed myself enough, I went to the kitchen to see my mother. I gave her his letter to read to show her how much I cared for her and trusted her. She dried her hands on her apron and sat down by the kitchen table to read his letter. Tears were also streaming down her face by the time she finished. Then she folded up the letter and gave it back to me – and took my hand and looked at the ring.

"It's very beautiful indeed," she said. "You must wear it with pride and always remember you father. He was a wonderful man. What a lovely gift he had for you, Rachel."

* * *

My father's funeral was the next day. Once the ceremony started, it was a machine one got stuck in. The only way out was through. It didn't seem to have much to do with my father's passing, at least not for me. I felt closest to him sitting the evening before in his worn chair in his room. But it wasn't until we were all standing around the deep pit in the ground and they were lowering my father's casket into it that it struck me – with that awful finality – that this was goodbye. I felt hot and cold all over and the earth turned. Then the black clad people and the grey autumn day and everything else was gone. I fainted for the first time in my life. When I opened my eyes, I found myself away from the group with my mother and Howard, my sister's husband bending over me.

"Rachel darling?" It was my mother's voice coming down a long dark tunnel. "Are you ok my darling?"

I smiled weakly.

My mother spoke softly and rapidly in Howard's ear. I

couldn't make out what she was saying. Then she kissed me on the cheek and went back to black clad group standing around the deep pit in the ground.

I struggled to get up. Howard was holding my hand, but I didn't want him too.

"Look Howard," I mumbled, "I'll be alright. I have to get back to my mother."

"Rachel, your mother just told me about your condition."

I looked at him in confusion. What was he talking about?

"She asked me to drive you home."

"But…"

He didn't let me finish, "There's no need for you to be here any longer. Your mother said she could manage without you. And you've got the baby to think of now."

"But it's my father!" I cried.

"Rachel, there's nothing more you can do now."

"But it's my father!" I struggled to free myself from his grip.

"Rachel, calm down. This is too much of a strain for you."

It was true. I felt exhausted; Howard was right. This was all too much for me. I went completely limp; I just wanted to get away from it all.

He helped me get up.

"Come Rachel, my car is over there."

I felt shaky and weak.

"But what about my mother?"

"Don't worry about your mother. Marlene will look after her. You just let me drive you home now."

He led me to his car.

I got in and sunk down in the seat. I just wanted to go to sleep and forget everything. Howard drove away and I was so exhausted, I dozed off immediately. When I woke up, we were parked in front of a modern looking office building. I looked around in confusion. I thought Howard was driving me back to my mother's house. Howard was coming around to my side of the car to open the door.

When he opened it, I said, "Where are we Howard? What's going on?"

"Rachel, this is where I have my office."

"What?"

"While you were sleeping I got to thinking that it's just not right you fainting like that, even if you are pregnant. I just want to check you, to make sure everything is all right."

I forgot Howard was a gynecologist.

"Oh come on Howard," I was really annoyed. "I'm all right. I just need some sleep."

"Well I just want to make sure." He was standing by the open door.

"It's just being pregnant and the shock of it all. Come on and drive me back to the house, I'm so sleepy."

"Rachel, just tell me – have you been to the doctor lately? Well have you?"

When I didn't reply he continued, "I'm not driving you back until you come to my office. It will only take a few minutes, Rachel. It's Sunday and the whole building is closed. Nobody is up there. I just want to take a blood test and make sure you are OK."

I couldn't believe my sister was married to this guy. He was such a creep. I imagined him spending his life poking around in women's insides. Well I sure as hell didn't feel like discussing my condition with him. But I had to be civil. After all, the guy was my half-sister's husband. I had to respect that, but he was such a creep. I knew he gave her the status she craved. But the thought of her going to bed with this creep – I wondered how she did it? I guess it was the price she had to pay for the lifestyle she wanted so badly. But sitting there listening to Howard talk, I couldn't help but wonder if she ever dreamed of really getting fucked front, back and sideways like I'd been fucked when I was in the south of France.

He had my hand and was pulling be out of the car.

"God Howard, my father just died. Is this really necessary?"

"Yes Rachel, now you just relax and come with me."

He led me through the lobby of the medical center and up to the second floor where he had his suite of offices. The place was deserted and spotlessly clean. He motioned me to take off my coat. Then he took off his and put on his white uniform. I followed him into his office and rolled up the sleeve of my black dress so he could do the blood test.

Suddenly he was acting very nervous.

"Rachel I want to examine you also. It could be anything you know, your fainting like that." He didn't look me in the eye.

"Where do you get all these crazy ideas from Howard, I'm perfectly fine."

"Healthy women don't faint. Now go in there and take your clothes off. There's a smock in there you can put on. Get up on the examination table and I'll be in with you as soon as I've washed my hands."

I started to feel sick. Was I really going to have this creep poking around inside me after all? If I hadn't been so tired and distraught thinking about my poor old father, I probably would have refused and left. But I didn't have the strength so I took off my clothes and got up on the table. Howard came in and put my legs up in position in the stirrups, spreading me wide open. He put on rubber gloves and stuck his fingers in me, pressing my abdomen. I closed my eyes and tried not to think about what he was doing.

After a couple of minutes, he said, "Everything's fine, you can sit up now Rachel."

But he didn't remove his fingers from my vagina, so how could I? And besides I still had my legs in the stirrups?

"Just take your legs out of the stirrups and sit up." He said; his voice strangely flat.

I did as he said and propped myself up on my elbows. "Aren't you going to remove your fingers Howard?"

"No Rachel, my fingers are right where I've wanted them to be for a very long time."

What? I thought, not believing what I just heard; I was stunned.

With his other arm, he grabbed hold of me around my waist and pressed me towards him.

"Let me go!" I said and tried pulling away, but he held me tight.

"Why should I, you little slut?"

I froze.

"What difference does it make to you – one man more or less? You've had so many, haven't you?" He was breathing hard and still holding me tightly.

"You probably don't even know who the father of the brat inside you is... well do you?"

When I didn't answer, he laughed. "See, I knew it. So what difference does it make to you? One man more or less. I want to fuck you Rachel, really fuck you."

"You're hurting me Howard, please stop it!"

But he didn't let go; instead he pushed his fingers into me harder. "Don't try that soft voice on me. I've wanted you for years, but you never looked at me, did you Rachel? Well now you're going to have to because I'm not letting you go."

"But Howard, I'm pregnant!"

"Yes, and I'm a gynecologist so I know for a fact that sex poses no danger for the fetus, especially in the early stages of pregnancy. And you can't be more than eight weeks pregnant."

I went limp trying to process what was going on.

To think that Howard had finally freaked out! It was probably the first time in his whole life. And I knew he couldn't possibly have planned this because he didn't know I would faint or that I was pregnant or that my mother would ask him to drive me home. It dawned on me that I really should give him a gold medal instead of fighting him.

That was when bad pussy took over and I hear myself saying, "Howard, if that's what you think about me, why don't you give me a chance to really show you my stuff?"

His jaw dropped and he stared at me with a look of bewilderment on his face.

"That sounds like whore talk."

"Well isn't that what you just said I was? If you really want to fuck me, you're going to have to take your fingers out."

He thought about what I said and withdrew his fingers slowly.

"Why don't you get undressed Howard?" I said laying it on really thick. For some reason, the situation made me remember how I'd done it in Nice with that awful German. If I could do it with Felix whatever-his-name-was, I could do it with creepy Howard Sloane.

"Don't you ever think about what your husband would do if he knew what you're really like?"

When I heard these words, the moment of inspiration passed and I went cold. "I think I better get dressed and go home," I said and started getting down from the table.

"Oh no you don't!" He said, blocking me. "You can't tease me like that and then just walk away." Then he began touching me and to my great surprise, instead of struggling, I just let him. For some reason, I didn't care. He stroked my breasts and then pinched my nipples as if testing the waters. Then he bent forward and took one of my nipples in between his teeth. At that moment, I felt his intense desire for me starting to turn me on. It was fascinating to watch and I found it (and him) both exciting and repulsive at the same time. It was bewildering. So much so, that I just sighed and lay back on the table, which made it easy for him to do what he wanted.

He let go of my nipple and moved downwards, kissing my belly hungrily and making his way down towards my pussy. "Oh

Rachel, please let me have you, please don't make me wait any longer," he moaned as he buried himself in my pussy, kissing and licking me excitedly.

"OK Howard, come here," I said softly, pulling him up and motioning for him to crawl up on top of me. He quickly took off his trousers and mounted me. The table wasn't comfortable and he was heavier than I expected, but his passion was real even though it was obvious from his clumsiness that he wasn't a man of experience. So I helped him enter me. But once inside me, he found his rhythm and was soon thrusting back and forth vigorously, sighing "Oh Rachel, oh." His hunger and desire were so real and compelling, that it made my hips do their little dance until he couldn't contain himself any longer. And when finally, he reached the point of no return, I let go too and came with him, amazed that I managed to make it with such a creep. But oh, what the hell I thought; a good orgasm was a good orgasm.

When he got up, he didn't look at me but grabbed his clothes and left the room. I waited for a while but when he didn't come back, I got dressed and went back to his office. He was fully dressed, gazing out the window.

"Rachel," he said hesitantly.

I went over to him.

"Rachel, please don't hate me for this," he said; he was having difficulty looking at me.

"Why should I hate you?"

He didn't reply.

"Come on Howard, don't be dumb. What should I hate you for? For being a man? For feeling what you feel?"

"You don't know how long I've wanted you. And today… well suddenly you were here… and I don't know… something inside me just went click."

"Forget the explanations, will you… You enjoyed yourself didn't you?"

"How can you think like that Rachel and be so free? I just

don't get it."

"Look Howard, I just want to go home now, ok? I'm tired."

"But I want a woman like you, Rachel."

He grabbed a hold of my arm.

"Then go out and find one."

"But what about Marlene? She's your sister – don't you care about her at all?"

"Look if you're not going to take me home, I'll go by myself." I grabbed my purse and walked toward the door.

He rushed after me. "Of course I'll take you home. Just let me kiss you one more time before we go." He pushed me up against the wall. "I could do it again you know." He started feeling my breasts.

"Oh no you don't!" I removed his hands. "Enough is enough."

"Take off your clothes and let me look at you."

"What are you thinking, man! Marlene and mother are going to start wondering where we are. You're going to make a mess of your life." I'd been a sentimental fool to let this creep fuck me in the first place.

He tore at my dress.

"I don't care Rachel, I want you." He was going to throw it all overboard. He pressed me against the wall and was moaning and kissing me. I squirmed and struggled to get away from him but he was stronger. I pushed against him and lifted up my knee and inserted it between us. Still he didn't let go, so I pushed up with my knee and kicked him firmly away from me. He stumbled backwards with a wild look on his face. I opened the door out to the hallway but he plunged after me and grabbed my arm.

I would have screamed but the building was deserted.

"You bitch," he cried, out of control, "teasing me like that!" He was still holding onto my arm with this crazy look on his face. I struggled to free myself from his grip.

"Bitch!" he cried again.

Then he swung out and hit me with this clinched fist on the

side of my face right by my eye. I was so shocked by the blow that I just stood there for a moment, frozen. When he realized what he'd done, he let go of me and crumpled down into a heap on the floor, sobbing. I rushed down the hall and stumbled into the elevator. Once I was down on the ground floor, I ran out of the building and down the street. I hurried around the corner and kept going until I was sure he wasn't following me. Fortunately for me, I had my purse.

When I was some blocks away, I took out my mirror and looked at my eye. It was already swelling and would be a real shiner by the time I got back to my mother's house. Oh what a mess! How would I ever explain this black eye to them? My only hope was to get back to the house before my sister and mother returned. I could go to bed and pretend I was sleeping.

But I knew that wouldn't work. Too much time had passed. They must be back at the house already. What could I do? Go back and tell them what? They knew Howard was supposed to drive me home. How could I face my sister? She'd guess right away what happened. I walked on in turmoil, not knowing what to do.

Finally I decided to call the house to see if anyone was home; my sister answered and I hung up. No I couldn't go back, not for a while. I had to think up a story. Maybe if I waited long enough, Marlene would be gone by the time I got back.

There was a drugstore on the corner so I went in and ordered coffee and a roll. I bought the New York Times and tried to read for a while but I couldn't concentrate. My mind was in turmoil trying to figure out what to do. Finally when I thought enough time had passed and that my sister would be gone, I took a cab back to my mother's house. It was getting dark outside. My mother was looking out the living room window as the cab pulled up. When she saw me getting out of the cab, she ran out the front door with a worried look on her face.

When she saw my face, she froze.

"Where's Marlene?" I cried.

"In the house... what...?"

Before she could say more I said, "I had some trouble with Howard and he hit me. I didn't come home sooner because of Marlene. I was hoping she'd be gone by now."

Marlene was coming out the front door in a big hurry.

"Momma, I'm going to tell her I was wandering around town feeling sad and didn't notice I'd ended up in a bad neighborhood until some punks started hassling me. You've got to back me up." I put my head on my mother's shoulder and pretended to cry.

Marlene was besides us. "My God, what's happened?"

"Come, come, let's get her inside the house," my mother said.

"Where is Howard?" my sister was looking at my swollen eye, "Rachel what happened to you?"

Looking at my sister made it easy to lie and cry. "I had a run in with some punks in the city!"

"Oh my God? Where were you, Rachel?" she was out of herself, trying to make sense of what I was saying, "I thought you were with Howard? I thought he was going to drive you home?"

"Marlene will you go get some ice cubes for Rachel's eye right this minute," my mother said as she opened the front door. "Can't you see she's in no condition to talk just yet? And besides, Rachel's pregnant."

My sister was so stunned by this new piece of information that she gasped and ran for the kitchen.

"Rachel," my mother continued, "you can tell me what happened later. I want to send Marlene home first."

Leaning on my mother I stumbled into the bedroom and pulled off my torn dress before my sister could see it. My mother pushed it under the bed just as my sister came back to the room with some ice cubes wrapped in a dish towel. She gave them to my mother who pressed them on my swollen check and eye. My sister stared at me but didn't say a word.

Isabel got up and said, "Rachel honey you must be exhausted.

You go to sleep now. We can talk about all this later."

"Thanks," I said, taking the ice pack and crawling further down under the blanket.

"I just don't understand what happened," my sister was saying.

My mother was drawing the curtains.

"I mean you were supposed to be with Howard. We just couldn't understand where the two of you had been all this time..." she said.

My mother pushed Marlene gently out the door. "Let's leave Rachel alone for now. She can tell us everything later... Just call me sweetheart if there is anything you need... Try to get some sleep." She closed the door but I could hear my sister's voice as they walked down the hall...."Mother I don't like it, I don't like it one bit..."

* * *

When I woke up, my mother was sitting on the end of the bed gazing out the window. She looked exhausted.

"Have I been sleeping long?" I asked her.

"Yes sweetheart, you actually slept all evening and all night," she looked at her watch, "It's almost noon now... you must have been really exhausted."

She was looking at me carefully, sizing me up. "You are a beautiful woman, Rachel, even with that black eye... will you tell me honestly what's going on? Marlene has worked herself up into a tizzy. We both thought Howard was going to bring you home."

"Everything's so confusing," I said slowly sitting up in the bed. "I just don't know how to explain."

"Well why don't you just begin at the beginning?"

I laughed, "The beginning of what?"

"Well let's just start with yesterday. You fainted at the funeral and I asked Howard to drive you home. I told him you were pregnant because he's a gynecologist. What happened then?"

I knew I couldn't tell her the truth. We had just buried my father and she was still reeling from shock and grief. So how could I possibly tell her what happened with Howard? It would have been difficult enough under normal circumstances, but now – no – no way.

So I knew I'd have to make up something quick. And it would have to be good because my mother was no dope.

I hemmed and hawed a bit and then plunged in. "Well after we left the funeral, I fell asleep in the car and when I woke up, I discovered that Howard had driven me to his clinic instead of back to the house. When I asked him what was going on, he said he was worried about me fainting like that and wanted to examine me to make sure I was alright. You know – him being a gynecologist and all. When I refused, he got upset so I left and wandered around the city a bit."

She listened quietly without taking her eyes off me and without interrupting.

"And the black eye…" she said slowly. "How did you get that?"

"After I wandered around for a while, I suddenly realized I wasn't sure where I was. It was a neighborhood I didn't recognize and pretty lousy at that. And then all of a sudden I had these two punks hassling me, one on either side of me, trying to touch me. I tried walking faster to get away, but one of them grabbed my arm. That really scared me so I screamed for help. That's when the other one slugged me. Then they just ran away. It was pretty scary… like I said…"

My mother took my hand, "But Rachel darling, that's not what you said yesterday when you got out of the cab! When you got out of the cab, you said it was Howard who hit you!"

The room went silent. My mother was silent, waiting for my reply.

At that very moment, the phone on my father's desk rang.

I sighed with relief. Saved in the knick of time!

She picked up the phone as I thanked my lucky stars. I'd forgotten I'd told her yesterday that Howard hit me. Phew. Now how was I going to get out of that? My brain was furiously trying to figure out a plausible explanation – one she would believe. So I wasn't really listening to what she was saying until she said, "Why yes, as a matter of fact she's right here. Just a minute."

I looked up in surprise as she passed the phone to me.

Who could it be?

I took the receiver.

"Hello?"

"Hi Rachel, it's me, Kenny."

"Kenny?" At first I was a total blank, but then I remembered the voice, "Kenny!" I exclaimed in delight, "but it can't be you!"

"Yes it is, baby!" I felt my face light up like a Christmas tree.

"Where are you... how did you know I was here?"

"Whoa babe, whoa... slow down a minute."

I laughed.

"Well I was out on the Island visiting my folks today and they mentioned that your old man had just passed away. So I figured you'd be back for his funeral. It's been a long time, hasn't it baby?"

"Yeah Kenny... it's been a long, long time." I just couldn't believe it. Was it really Kenny? It must have been ten or twelve years since I saw him last. He was my first really big flame, the guy who first took me to Europe, the guy who... "But we have a million things to talk about," I stammered. "I just can't believe it."

"Yeah Rachel, we've got to get together. Look babe... let me see... what time is it? It's almost noon. OK look honey, I'll come pick you up at about two, OK?"

When I said yes, he hung up.

I just sat there stunned, staring at the phone in my hand.

Kenny! I turned to my mother, feeling more than slightly dazed. I felt like smiling, but of course I couldn't and didn't when I saw the look on her face.

"Don't tell me that was really Kenny Davenport?"

The way she said it reminded me of the fact that my parents were never particularly fond of Kenny.

"Yes it was."

"But I thought you'd lost contact with him."

"I thought so too. Look mom, he's going to pick me up at two."

"But Rachel," my mother said, "we just buried your father and we're in mourning, you know that. You can't just leave... and besides the whole family is coming later this afternoon, including Jerry's brothers and their wives and Marlene and Howard. They'll all wonder where you are."

"Yeah I know momma," I said, taking her hand and patting it gently as the obvious way out flashed through my mind. "But you know it'll only be trouble if I'm here when Howard and Marlene come."

I knew by saying that I was giving things away and admitting it was Howard who hit me, but it was the only good excuse I could think of. She kept on looking at me intently and I held my breath, afraid she was going to ask me again what really happened yesterday with Howard.

"I supposed you're right Rachel," my mother said and sighed. "I'm really too tired to think about it anymore." She really looked worn out.

I hugged her and she started to cry.

"Oh dearest momma," I said and held her. Now it was her turn to sob like a baby. So I just sat there and let her cry, rocking her back and forth.

When she finally stopped, she squeezed my hand gently and said, "Now get out of here and take a shower. And see if you can't cover up that black eye before Kenny gets here."

"If it's any comfort to you at all, I just want you to know that Kenny is one of the best people I've ever known. He's got a heart of gold momma. Really."

"Whatever you say," she said sighing deeply. "Just remember you're pregnant and will be soon going back to Amsterdam."

But I wasn't listening. I was smiling inside and happy; soon I was going to be seeing one of my dearest friends.

* * *

I decided to wait for Kenny outside by the front driveway to save my mother the hassle of having to meet him on that day. And to tell the truth, I was relieved to have something else to think about besides the death of my father. Maybe it wasn't proper to feel this way, but I felt my grief was my own private business. I desperately needed to get away from the house and all the people who would soon be showing up with solemn expressions on their faces. I didn't want to share my grief with anyone except my mother. And to think Kenny Davenport was my way out, my excuse! So there I was, waiting on the front lawn, out of my mourning clothes and back in my jeans, sweater and white jacket. I hoped he would still think I looked good. So many years had gone by since I saw him last. Kenny had to be at least 40.

A beat-up grey Ford pulled up and Kenny sprang out of the car. I ran madly towards him. We embraced and embraced. Neither of us could believe it. Finally we let go and looked at each other, both a little afraid to see what time had done to the other.

"Rachel, you haven't changed a bit! Unless... well... you look even better than before!"

"Oh come on Kenny!"

"No kidding, you look great. But whatever did you do to your eye?"

"I'll tell you later. Come on, let's get out of here!"

He winked and we got in the car. As he started the engine, I looked at him again. He looked the same too, but definitely older. His jet black hair was streaked with grey and there were lots of wrinkles around his eyes as if some sorrow had followed him. My heart ached for him, the dear man. I loved him so.

"Where to?" I asked.

"You remember our special spot?" he smiled as he turned the car around.

"Yeah," I smiled at the memory.

"Who knows, the hole in the fence might still be there!" he laughed.

"We can try," I leaned over and kissed him on the cheek.

My parent's house was at the end of a dead end street and running all along the side of our house and the other houses on the street was a big wire fence with an exclusive golf course on the other side. A few blocks from my house, Kenny and I had found a hole in the fence many, many years ago when we were just teenagers. The hole in the fence was hidden behind some bushes and many evenings when it wasn't too cold and we wanted to be alone and talk, we'd slip through the fence and sit under the trees along the fairways of the golf course and talk. It was our secret entrance to our own special land. So we jumped for joy when we discovered the hole in the fence still there.

"Can you believe it?" I laughed when we moved the bushes apart.

"Yes I guess it's still here because of all the bushes. Nobody's ever discovered it!"

"Don't you think there might be other young lovers who've discovered it?"

"Sure, why not! Do you think we're the only Kenny and Rachels to come out of this crazy suburb?"

"It's fun to think of, really," I smiled. "Others sneaking through here like we used to do."

We crept through and walked hand in hand down through the

trees until we found the perfect spot to sit. The afternoon sun was warm and strong and there were still a few golfers out on the fairways. We took care to keep out of sight.

We talked peacefully for a long time. The early evening came and had that kind of clear sharpness and quiet that only comes with fall. Everything seemed in perfect harmony sitting there under the softly swaying beeches and maples that lined the fairways. It seemed almost as if time had turned back upon itself. We were, if only for a few moments, back again in that time when life was just beginning for us both, when we were both filled with a burning desire to get away from home and experience the world. But now, time had moved on. We were both older and had both sustained grievous wounds which neither of us would have thought possible back in that magical time.

I wondered if we had known back then if we would have done differently?

Kenny told me about his two kids who lived with their mother in Seattle. At least they lived in same town as Kenny so he got to see them often. I didn't even know he lived there – we'd been out of touch for so long – but when I heard, it made me realize that we were living on opposite sides of the planet. Strange to think two people could be so far apart who once had been so close.

"Come Rachel and sit here with me," he pulled me into the crack of his arm like he used to in the old days. "I'm not going to have you around for very long... so when's the baby due?"

"Mid-May I think... I'm not quite sure."

We sat in silence for a while. "Will you write to me again now that I've found you?" I asked quietly, "I couldn't bear to lose you again."

"But you already have lost me, you know that. And you know I'm terrible at writing letters. What's there to say anyway?"

"Oh you know I'd just like to know you're OK, that's all."

He had this strange look on his face when I said that.

"You are OK, aren't you Kenny?" He seemed far away.

"Look Rachel," he moved suddenly, breaking the spell, "let's go see Mike Dorsey. You remember him, don't you? Old friend of mine from way back?"

I was surprised.

"But Kenny, why now? It's so nice here."

"Come on, I've got a little business with him, it will only take a few minutes." Suddenly he was irritated, nervous.

"Okay, okay," I said, getting up and brushing off my clothes, wondering at his sudden change in mood. Up until then he's been so relaxed, now he was all jumpy and wired. I noticed his hands trembled as he lit a cigarette.

We walked back to the car in silence. I felt sad because Kenny was so different, changed. He'd never be the same Kenny I'd known and loved years ago. Too much had happened. He was worn and wounded though he tried valiantly to put on a happy face. When we first fell in love, it wasn't only sex we shared; we shared a common background, a common language, a common understanding. Now, years later, we still shared those bonds, but there were also many years of experience on opposite sides of the planet that we didn't share.

And I knew there was something else, but I wasn't sure what.

He didn't say a word as we drove towards the city.

Somewhere in Queens I asked, "Does Mike Dorsey live here? I thought he was from Port Washington like you."

"He's got a place in Queens now."

"What's he doing these days?"

"Oh come on Rachel, can't you see I'm in a bad way? Just let me concentrate on getting us there."

It was beginning to dawn on me what was going on so I kept quiet.

When we stopped at a traffic light, Kenny turned to me and took my hand, "Look babe, I'll be okay again soon. I just forgot the time out there, that's all."

I smiled at him, but my heart ached. Maybe it would have been better if I'd never seen him again. That way I could have kept my magical picture of my first true love.

Mike Dorsey lived on an evil looking street in an evil smelling building. Kenny made no comment, he was in a hurry. We had stayed and talked too long on the pleasant fairways of the golf course. I understood that now.

Kenny barged into Mike's apartment as soon as Mike opened the door.

"Jesus, you're late man," Mike said.

Kenny was sweating. "Yeah," he mumbled, "you remember Rachel? Now fix me up quick; I've really got the shakes man."

"Rachel, sit down with my friends," Mike motioned to two black guys sitting on a very worn-out leather sofa watching TV. "Otis and Jesse, this is Rachel." Mike led Kenny away and I heard him saying to Kenny, "It's cool man, it's cool. Just come into my bedroom."

Jesse and Otis said "hi" and I sat down feeling very deflated. I was happy I didn't have to talk to these dudes. I needed to think. My trip to America was turning out to be a real eye-opener. It was bad enough my father had died, but to get messed over by my brother-in-law and then find out that my first true love was doing himself in with heroin, well that really took the cake. Kenny and I had been into grass and hash and all that stuff back then, but so had everybody else been. But what made him go on? Had he seen it all too clearly and been unable to function after that or what? There was so much about Kenny I didn't know.

I wished in my heart of hearts I hadn't seen this.

What was taking them so long anyway?

Mike barged back into the room in a panic. "Jesus! Get in here Jes, Otis... I think this dude might just have OD'd."

I went icy cold. Jesse and Otis jumped up.

Mike was shouting, "What kind of motherfucking shit you bringing in here?"

"I don't know man, cool it," Jesse was saying, "it's from our usual."

"Let's walk the motherfucker!" Mike was shouting and they dragged Kenny into the living room. Otis was slapping Kenny's face – he seemed completely gone, his head hanging down, his face ashen grey.

"Walk man, walk!" And they walked him and they walked him. I sat completely frozen, in shock, unable even to pray. Was this really happening? Was this really Kenny, the man I'd known who had so much promise? Was he going to die too? My father had just died, but he was old and it was natural for him to go. But Kenny wasn't old, he was just wounded. God I wished I could change things.

They walked him and walked him.

An eternity passed.

Suddenly Kenny moaned a bit and we heaved a collective sigh of relief. At least we had a chance.

"Keep walking him man," Otis commanded, "he ain't through this yet." Otis sat down by my side while Jesse and Mike kept walking Kenny back and forth.

"What did he do man?" Otis asked Mike.

"Look he said he was upset and needed a little extra to make it through. How the hell could I know what was going on?"

I put my head in my hands and started to cry.

Otis patted my knee. "Look honey, it ain't your fault. The man is grown up, can't you see that?"

I looked up. "Will he be okay?"

"Yeah, I think so. We is lucky this time, real lucky."

Kenny was showing more signs of life, some leg movements and mumbling. I got up and said to Jesse that I would replace him. Mike and I kept on walking him around and around. He was coming to.

"Gotta piss something terrible," was the first thing he said. Mike and me steered him towards the bathroom. He stumbled and bumbled and wasn't even aware that I was standing there with him. He couldn't open his pants and Mike did it for him. His shrunken penis flopped out and he peed and peed and peed. It took forever and I kept thinking the whole time it was a crushing way to see the penis of a man you once loved. It was limp and lifeless and totally sexless. I think Mike suddenly realized what I was thinking. He called in Jesse and told me to go back into the living room.

I had to get out of there.

Mike and Jesse came back into the room and kept walking Kenny.

Mike said to Otis, "Take the keys to my car and drive Rachel home." Then he said to me, "Look Rachel, Kenny ain't gonna be no good to nobody for a while. It just causes you pain to see him like this and you can't help him no way... so just get out of here."

I was grateful Mike knew I had to get away.

"Mike, I can get home myself," I said as I stood up, but I wasn't too sure about it.

"Look honey, this neighborhood might be tricky for a lady looking like you do, so you just let Otis here drive you on home."

I never liked Mike Dorsey before, but the years had given him a sympathetic edge. I was grateful. I hugged him goodbye and kissed Kenny on the cheek. He didn't notice. "Take care of Kenny, will you?"

"He's gonna be okay... now you get out of here woman!"

I stumbled out of the apartment and into the car without really noticing that the night had become wet with a slow, steady drizzle. Otis was the perfect companion, he didn't say a word.

I slid down in my seat and gazed blankly out through the window at the rain splattered city streets. I couldn't place myself in the landscape; Kenny's pals lived in a part of the city I didn't know. And with the events of the last few days piling up in my brain and the city passing before my eyes, I felt kind of overwhelmed to put it mildly. There was just so much going on, both externally and internally. Was any of this real? I felt strangely cut off from my surroundings. Yet outside the rain battered the windows in the red glow of the traffic light and people crossed the street right in front of us. People no different from me. People who were perhaps no wiser, but certainly no worse. Why couldn't I just relax and enjoy the changing scenery of life? When I was younger, I could get into the raw energy of the city without judging, but now I couldn't. Now I felt locked in a dream I couldn't relate to. My father's death, dear, dear Kenny, the city I loved so much… what was wrong with me? Or was it just the overload of emotions that was causing my whole system to shut down? I felt wiped out, wasted, empty and exhausted. All I wanted to do was disappear from the face of the earth.

I couldn't forget the pain in Kenny's eyes when he was standing on the edge.

"Rachel," Otis broke the silence as he swung onto the open road taking us out to the Island, "you can't let these things get to you, you know that, don't you?"

"Yeah, I guess so," I sighed, "it's just I was at my father's funeral yesterday and it seemed nearly too much if I was gonna have to bury Kenny too."

"Oooh…" he replied softly, "I didn't know."

"Know? How could you? You see I live in Europe Otis, and have just came over for my father's funeral. I didn't even know Kenny was in town. I mean Kenny was my old man about 12 years ago and I haven't seen him since."

Otis didn't say anything.

Now the tears were streaming down my face.

"Oh come on babe, it'll pass. You is strong."

"But why Otis, why? Why does it have to be like this?"

"You asking the wrong man babe, the wrong man." Otis turned on the radio and the strong music vibrated through the car. It was his way of saying there was no sense in pursuing this discussion any further. It wasn't going to lead us anywhere because if it did, if it could, he wouldn't be driving me home through this city through this universe at this very moment in this very condition. If it could be different, it would be different and it wasn't. We were just two strangers thrown together on a rainy night and the best we could do was gather what comfort we could from each other and the music. Let the dead lie in peace and the rain and music wash away the pain if only for a little while.

I smiled.

He was right. My father was dead and nothing could bring him back. And Kenny was alive.

When we got back to my mother's house, I wanted to thank him for just being there, but all I could say was, "Thanks for the ride man, thanks a lot." I kissed him on the cheek and from the kindness in his eyes I knew he was a true friend.

"Don't let 'em get you down," was all he said.

His car was gone before I reached the front door of the darkened house.

I was relieved to see the house was dark. That meant everyone had gone home! There was only one small light on in the living room; that was all. I was cheered by the thought that there would be no one to face, no one to talk to, no lingering guests, not even my mother.

I was so exhausted.

I looked up, hoping to see a single star, one that would give me comfort, but there were no stars to be seen, only soft rain which felt cool on my face. I took a deep breath, put my key in the lock and opened the front door. I closed the door behind me softly, not wanting to wake my mother. I leaned back against the shut door and sighed. From where I was standing I could see into the living room and my eyes quickly found the one small lamp that was lit next to my father's favorite chair. I shivered. My brother-in-law Howard was sitting there. Howard! What was he doing there? He leapt up and sprang towards me before I could think or move. And in a flash, he was upon me, pressing me deep into the massive oak front door, kissing me passionately on the neck. I struggled to get away, but couldn't.

He was talking rapidly as if a volcano was pent up inside him. "Rachel, you've got to understand, Rachel, I just had to see you. You mustn't be angry at me. Rachel." He took my face in his hands.

I felt my blood turn to ice.

"Where's my mother?" I asked.

"She's sleeping. Don't worry about her."

"What do you mean, don't worry about her?"

"I gave her a sedative, she was so upset."

"Upset?" I tried to get away from him, but he was stronger. "Tell me what happened to my mother, Howard. Tell me." I couldn't hide the hysteria in my voice.

"I don't know. It happened all of a sudden, about eight this evening. She just broke down."

"What do you mean just broke down?" It didn't sound like my mother.

"I don't know. Your Uncle Jake made some stupid remark, it wasn't anything special, but it set her off and she started crying. And she just kept on crying and crying and wouldn't stop. So I sent everyone home and gave her a sedative, a strong one. She won't wake up until tomorrow Rachel, I promise you... oh Rachel."

"My mother..."

"She's fine Rachel, don't worry, she's sleeping peacefully."

"I want to see her." I thought he must be mad.

"No Rachel. No. You don't want to disturb her."

I struggled to free myself but he kissed me again and pressed himself against me. I was so tired, so washed out. I tried to fight back but was so exhausted all I could feel was my knees shaking.

I felt like falling down on the floor in a heap but his hands were already inside my jacket finding their way under my t-shirt. I could feel his hardness as he pressed himself again me.

"Come Rachel," his voice was husky, "Come let me put you to bed. You must be tired my darling. It's been a long day. Let me help you."

My brain couldn't comprehend more after all that had happened. It was as if the overwhelm of life just washed over me and my resistance to Howard or anything for that matter crumbled before the tide.

I let him lead me down the hallway towards my father's study where I'd been sleeping. Everything about the house was dark and silent, like a tomb. Was this all a dream? And if it was, why couldn't I wake up? I felt myself panic. What should I do, scream, holler? But who would hear me if I did? Should I kick him, bite, shout? Should I throw one of my mother's fine Chinese lamps at his head? I was so tired, so exhausted and he was so full of fire and desire, it made him strong, stronger than he'd ever been in his life I thought. And there I was, all alone with this maniac in my mother's house. If I screamed there was no one around to hear me except my mother and I just couldn't bear the thought of what would happen if she woke up. Not after all she'd been through the last few days.

I felt feverish, hot all over; I knew I was trapped.

What could I do?

There was no way out.

And what difference did it make anyway? Wasn't it just yesterday that I'd let Howard fuck me? Me and my cocky little self who wasn't thinking about consequences... Bad pussy letting him have his way with me? So what difference would it make now? One more little fuck? Or two? Me the great seeker of freedom and all that! Why should I care now?

We were in my father's study, the bed was already made. He was taking off my white jacket, then my t-shirt and bra. I just stood there like a little girl, completely still and silent, letting him do what he wanted. I was obsessed with the thought of not waking my mother. And then I thought thank God Kenny's alive. Thank God! Howard was undoing my jeans; they were tight but I didn't help him. He struggled to pull them down. And then he was pulling my panties down too, touching me and all I could do was stand there. Dead like stone. And there I was, completely naked, except for my boots. He pushed me gently down on the bed and then pulled off my boots and then my socks, jeans and panties. I just lay there, stark naked, staring up at the ceiling.

I was cold but I didn't cover myself. I simply couldn't move. I was frozen like a deer, caught in the headlights of a car on a deserted road. With nowhere to run.

So I lay there, perfectly still.

Waiting for my fate, knowing this was my destiny.

He stood there, undressing quickly, talking all the time. Blabbering, saying things like, "I knew you would understand Rachel, I knew you would. I never wanted to hurt you. If only you knew how much I want you. I'm sorry about the black eye." Now he was next to me, stroking my hair, stroking my face around my black eye. He was trembling. "Oh my darling, I've been waiting for you for so long, for so many years... My darling Rachel, my darling." He climbed up on top of me, smothering me with kisses. I felt absolutely nothing. I was as empty as a dried out well. Empty. Dead. The past two days had taken their toll on me. Life had taken its toll. I didn't move. He spread my legs apart and went down and licked me, trying to make me wet, knowing he couldn't enter me as dry as I was. When he realized I wasn't wet enough, he took a tube of lubricant out of the pocket of his pants which were lying on the floor. Then he spread me wide enough to cover me with the gel. I let him. He could do what he wanted. I didn't care anymore. I had surrendered. Let go. Life could do whatever it wanted with me. It was as if I wasn't there anymore. It was as if I no longer existed. And when he was satisfied that I was wet enough, he climbed back on top of me and entered me. I felt him quiver, his desire was that fierce. Mine was non-existent so I made no sound or movement, but he didn't seem to mind. He was fucking his fantasy anyway so what difference did it make what I felt. All I knew was that I was floating somewhere in a darkened room, being fucked by who was it? Too many men had passed this way lately... It was eerie... as if I had found myself somewhere, in some space, where I myself had disappeared. There was just no me anymore to be fucked and yet the fucking went on anyway. And some part of me knew it, some part of me knew the hard fact of the man on top of me, the man who was all over me, who was kissing, licking, sucking, heaving, sighing, sweating and penetrating me over and over again until there was nothing left but wetness, semen, darkness.

When he was finally done, I slept. Or maybe I slept even before he was done. The sleep of a total zero.

Either way it didn't matter.

* * *

When I woke up the next morning, the sun was streaming in the window. I was covered and all alone in my bed. The room around me and my clothes and everything were in perfect order.

It was as if nothing had happened.

Maybe it was all a dream. But I knew it wasn't.

Graphic memories flooded back. My mouth tasted bitter and funny.

The old clock on my father's desk said quarter past 11.

I got up and wobbled out to the bathroom and brushed my teeth. Then I splashed cold water on my face and examined my black eye. I still had quite a shiner.

Then I remembered my mother – and my heart jumped. *Where was she? Was she okay?* I grabbed my father's bathrobe from behind the bathroom door and threw it around me.

The house was quiet, too quiet, it frightened me.

Panicking, I forgot all about my own troubles and ran down the hall to my parents' bedroom.

Phew she was there, alive, breathing, sitting half-propped up in her bed, gazing out the open window at the rain-swept garden. I sighed with relief.

Outside her window, the old red beech tree swayed gently in the wind and was making soft, comforting sounds. The light flickered and danced through the shifting leaves. I had loved that wonderful tree ever since I was a child and it was still there, still standing in the wind and weather.

It was the first time I'd ever seen my mother sit so still. I went over to the bed and sat down besides her and took her hand. She smiled at me wanly and turned to gaze out the window again. I wished I could help her, do something to ease her pain.

"Mother may I crawl in with you?"

She smiled very gently and lifted the covers by her side, "Why of course my darling, that would be so nice."

I snuggled in besides her, but this time, instead of her taking me in her arms, I took her in mine. She didn't protest and snuggled deeper into my embrace. We sat there like that without speaking for a long time. I stroked her hair softly, realizing that for the first time in my life, it was now my turn to put my troubles aside and comfort her as best I could.

Tears were streaming down her cheeks, "You know all my happiest memories are here in this house, "she said her voice quivering. "You grew up here, and well, all the good years I've had with your father... He was such a dear man."

"It's okay to cry momma."

I held her tighter.

And cry she did, that kind of deep agonizing weeping that comes from the depths of one's soul. I tried to help her by loving her. But is there any comfort for such hurts in this world?

Nothing can turn back the clock or bring back the ones we love.

"I wish you didn't live so far away Rachel," she said still weeping. "All of a sudden the house feels so big and I feel so alone." She cried some more.

When she quieted down a bit, I said softly, "Well the truth is momma, I'm thinking about coming back to New York."

That got her attention.

She sat up straight and blew her nose.

"You're what?"

"I'm thinking about coming back."

Up until that moment, I hadn't told her I didn't love Jan anymore. In fact up until that moment I hadn't told her anything. My father had just died and there hadn't been time. "I don't know if I want to be with Jan anymore. I just don't think I can live the lie any longer."

When she didn't say anything, I continued. "Momma, the truth is I don't love him anymore," I said vehemently. "In fact, I think I'm beginning to hate him… everything about him. I'm just so sick of him, sick of everything, really! I don't know what I ever saw in him!" Now that I was telling her the truth, it all came pouring out. I was surprised at how angry and upset I was. "Ugh! I should have never asked him to come back! Never! What was I thinking? But I didn't know what to do! Being pregnant and all. And Stefan didn't want me… It was all such a mess and I felt so lost…"

Now it was my turn to cry.

My mother put her arms around me and rocked me back and forth.

"Oh momma, I've made a mess out of everything!" I said sobbing. "And everyone I talk to says I should get an abortion, but I can't… really I just can't… but I can't go on living that lie any longer either."

We were silent for a while.

"Well that's a bit of news…" she said slowly, "though now

that you actually say it, the truth is I guess I knew it all along. Or I should say I surmised you didn't love him anymore. But when you said you were going back to him, your father and I figured you were going to give it another try. So we didn't say anything and perhaps we were wrong to even suggest you going back to him when we met you in Nice."

The room was silent; I could hear the old beech tree outside swaying in the wind.

"Rachel darling," she was saying softly. "Why don't you just take Daniel and come back to New York and stay here with me, at least for a while. You can stay here for as long as you want, you know that."

"Thanks momma. That would be a big help... You know I really hate myself for getting myself into this mess."

"Come, come my dear. You shouldn't hate yourself for being human," she said. "We all make mistakes and to tell you the truth, your father and I never thought you and Jan were such a good match to begin with. And besides, marriage isn't always the easiest thing in the world even when you are a good match!"

"Yeah I know what you mean. But I never dreamed it would be so frustrating and uninteresting as it turned out. And the truth is Jan can just be so mean and small-minded – and I feel so trapped by it all. I often find myself thinking holy shit, is this really it? I mean is this really my life? I know it sounds dumb, but for a long time now I've been feeling like I'm always sacrificing myself and my own dreams to please either Jan or Daniel. But what about me? Don't I get to live a little?"

"Well darling, being a wife and a mother can be terribly frustrating at times" she said, "especially if you're smart and talented like you are and used to a high level of activity and stimulation. You've had a very exciting life Rachel. You had a good education and traveled a lot and had a lot of different boyfriends, so God knows it's understandable that you feel stuck at the moment with one small child and another on the way."

"It's not that I don't love Daniel."

"Oh I know, I know," my mother sighed, "but loving your son's got nothing to do with it. The reality is that a woman often ends up feeling like she's a doormat for everybody to step on, especially if she only does for her children and her husband and never for herself. When that happens, a day must come when all her pent-up desires finally come to the surface. And that seems to be what's happening to you Rachel – so all I can say is whether you stay with Jan or leave him, it's definitely time for you to start doing things for you and to start making a life for yourself again. I know it's easy for me to say, but once the baby's born and you're finished nursing, you've got to start building a life for yourself again. Go back to school, get your degree, or get a real job, something that really challenges you... Do something that makes a difference..."

"Oh momma, I know you're right... there's just so much I want to do, explore," I said, staring out the window. "But now I'm going to have another baby! It's just so damn frustrating! I feel like exploding sometimes!"

"Well it will be for a while, or at least until you can put the baby into daycare. But then my dear, you can do what you like. If you come back to New York, I'll help you in anyway I can. And even if you stay in Amsterdam, I'll still help you, you know that. But you must do something that really challenges you and interests you – something where you can use your talent and your brains, something productive, something exciting!"

"Something exciting – oh yes exciting," I said and sighed again. "Talking about exciting... having that affair with Stefan, well that was exciting, it really was. It made me feel so alive again just to be with him. It made me feel wanted, it made me feel seen for who I am. And the adventure of it... oh momma!" I wanted her to know the whole of it, the whole truth of at least that experience, so I told her. "Just being on the Riviera and the sex, the hot sex, well suddenly I felt alive again and life was fun.

It was like I got my life back... or so I thought... that was... until I found out I was pregnant!"

"Of course my darling, it makes perfect sense," she said stroking my hair. "A beautiful, talented, hot-blooded girl like you wants to feel life in her veins! It's only natural!"

"But when it turned out I was pregnant, Stefan didn't want me anymore! The bum wouldn't stand by me – even if it's probably his baby. It just isn't fair!"

"Now, now," she said, stroking my hair softly.

"Ugh, ugh, ugh," I added heatedly. "I'm so mad I don't know whether to laugh or cry when I think about it!"

And then I laughed – and when I did, she laughed too.

And then we looked at each other; each knowing the other would survive.

PART IV

AMSTERDAM

Good pussy bad pussy. Despite the traumatic events of New York and the deepening realization that all my actions had consequences, I also knew something else had awakened in me, something I'd never experienced before. A force, a power, a drive, an energy. Call it good pussy, call it bad pussy, call it whatever you will, but a life force had been awakened in me and I couldn't put it (her) back to sleep again. Right or wrong. Pregnant or not. She was awake! She was alive! She wanted to live. And she wanted more.

She, my pussy, was alive in me. I felt her moving in me, reaching out, right or wrong, pregnant or not. She wanted to taste and touch, to be tasted and touched. She wanted to feel the life force, the energy, moving in and through her. She wanted like liquid desire itself. She wanted because she was, life itself. She wanted because she was, the energy of life itself. And now that she – the genie – was out of the bottle, there was no putting her back again. She was untameable, wild; she wanted to be free, had to be free. Because she loved life, because yes, she was life itself. She was the life force in all of us… she was the creative power of the universe – and yes she was sex. Sex! Sex! Sexual! She was pure and beautiful and couldn't be kept down or locked up. And now she was awake in me, awake! A ravishing beauty, a hungry cunt, a wantingness for the essence of life. And what was that essence? It was the ecstasy of knowing my own soul, my own being, which was somehow alive and felt like frolicking in that stream of liquid desire that carries one on and on unto a state of orgasmic bliss, which was somehow like coming home and finding a peace that was beyond all comprehension… home, home, home. That's what I wanted, that's what she wanted, that's where she was taking me, taking me, taking me… and there was nothing, nothing I could do about it. No stopping her. No turning back now.

She was me and I was her.

And we were flying.

And my plane was approaching Amsterdam, and soon I'd be back. Landed again. Back with Jan again, back with my son again, back with my old life again. Back. But I knew, with a finality, a certainty that I'd never felt before, that I couldn't do it, couldn't go back, ever. No. Never. It – my life with Jan – was over. I couldn't do it anymore. Couldn't live the lie anymore. Couldn't do good pussy or nice mommy anymore, couldn't do housewife or second in command to him anymore. I'd have to get out, cost what it may. I'd have to break free, even if I was confused and pregnant and even if I couldn't see the way forward clearly. I'd have to do it anyway. Even if it was painful. Even if he went mad with rage. Whatever it was, I had to do it. Had to break free. Had to be me. Had to follow my heart. Once and for all. Now at least I had my mother; at least now I knew she'd help me. So it wasn't all that bad. I'd go back to New York and stay with her for a while. It couldn't be that difficult. All I had to do was break free and tell Jan.

But that – as I soon found out – was easier said than done.

* * *

Because there was just one small problem; I was afraid of Jan. Scared to death of how he'd react; scared of the fury I was sure I would unleash in him the moment he realized that even though I'd asked him to come back, I really didn't want him. That I had lied to him. Lied to him. Oh yes, that would make him furious, just furious. He'd call me a manipulative bitch and every other name in the book. And I wouldn't be able to deny it because he'd be right. So I'd end up cowering before him and he'd probably threaten me by saying he'd never let me have custody of Daniel. He'd used Daniel to manipulate me and make me cower before. Maybe he'd even hit me. He'd been close to doing it before, when he found out about Stefan. It was painful to contemplate and I was scared... yes terrified. So the thought of telling him was daunting indeed. It would take courage, lots of courage on my part – and for some reason I suddenly didn't feel that I had all that much. Why was it like that when I'd been so bold and ballsy before? All I had to do was tell him and then figure out the practicalities and cut loose. It was easy. Why was I making such a big deal of it? But then I'd think about his temper and the way he could rage at me, and I'd freeze up. There was just something about him, something about that authoritarian manner he had, that scared the shit out of me. So every time I thought I was ready to tell him, I'd chicken out again and the moment would pass.

But I knew I couldn't put it off forever. I'd made up my mind, so I'd have to do it sooner or later. I was going to go back to New York with Daniel and stay with my mother for a while. At least until the baby was born. So it was just a matter of telling him.

But for one reason or another, I kept putting it off and shaming and blaming myself for not speaking my truth, for being such a coward. Then finally, after I'd been home a little over two weeks, I felt ready. I felt I'd mustered up the courage to tell him. It had been a quiet morning and Jan had come home from the shop for lunch. We'd almost finished eating and I was feeling confident that now I could do it, say it. And then, just as I opened my mouth to tell him, the doorbell rang.

Jan got up and went to answer the door.

"Rachel," Jan called from the hallway, "come and see who's here. You won't believe it."

I was still in my bathrobe and got up moodily. I was just about to tell Jan I was leaving him and didn't want anybody coming in just then. I went to the door half-heartedly, took one look at our visitor and fainted.

When I opened my eyes I was lying in bed. Jan was sitting beside me and Howard was standing behind him. Howard! So it was true. Howard was in Amsterdam! I felt sick and panicky.

Jan was saying, "Rachel, are you okay?"

I didn't know what to say.

"I guess it was just too much of a surprise for you," Jan continued. "Howard wants to give you a little something to help you relax, okay? I think you should. You can just sleep. Don't worry I'll pick up Daniel."

Howard was already preparing an injection and Jan was rolling up the sleeve of my robe. I wanted to cry out and tell Jan to make Howard go away. But how could I? What would I say? How could I explain it? The needle went into my arm and the heaviness hit me. My eyelids felt like lead.

When I work up later, the first thing I was aware of was his hand on my breast. I didn't need to open my eyes to know who it was. He sensed I was coming around.

"Rachel?"

I opened my eyes and stared up into Howard's face. He was sitting besides me and he was naked.

"Where's Jan?"

"Oh Jan went back to work. I told him I would take care of you." He smiled.

He had already pulled back the covers and opened my bathrobe while I was sleeping. I was totally exposed and he leaned forward and kissed my belly. I struggled to free myself, but I was dazed from the sedative and my arms and legs felt like dead weights. He smothered me with hot kisses, one hand caressing my breasts, the other exploring and touching me down between my legs.

"Rachel," he mumbled, "I couldn't live without you." He moved down, licking me with his hungry mouth and then covering me with lubricant to make me wet enough so he could enter me. Obviously he was in a hurry. I struggled to wake up as he moved up and then he was over me, above me, bearing down on me, holding my hands down on the bed. I had to wake up. I had to.

"You changed my life," he said fervently. "I just had to have you one more time... I just had to..." I cried out in surprise as he thrust himself into me and started moving. But he didn't care; he just continued, thrusting himself deeper and deeper into me.

"You can't get away from me now… I've got you."

And he was right. I was too drugged to move.

I turned my face away and closed my eyes, still struggling to wake up.

What was he doing in Amsterdam?

In my bed?

Inside of me?

The room swam.

But despite my bewilderment, bad pussy started to respond to the sex and I felt myself becoming softer and wetter as he moved inside of me. And even in my drugged state, I sensed a change in his body; he was tighter and firmer than when I saw him last.

I heard myself moaning as hot tears of anger and confusion sprang from my eyes. And he kept on thrusting and thrusting with great force, deep inside me. And then surprisingly, he suddenly paused and slowed down and waited and moved around inside me gently and softly, deep inside me, waiting, lingering, in a way that was strangely thrilling. What was going on? Bad pussy was really awake now… intrigued. But I wasn't… All I could think was – was this really Howard, the man I so desperately despised? Yet despite my revulsion, I heard myself sighing and he, realizing the effect he was having on me, waited and then waited just a little longer, holding himself back with a sudden knowingness and softness… until it happened just as he had longed for and so desperately wanted … my body or I should say bad pussy opened to him; maybe against my will, but it was happening anyway and I was coming and coming hard and then and only then did he growl fiercely like an animal and let himself explode triumphantly inside me.

* * *

When I woke up later I got a shock, Jan was sitting besides me. But looking down at myself I realized I was under the covers. Howard was nowhere in sight.

"Are you feeling better now?" Jan asked.

"Jan, I don't want Howard around," I said vehemently, sitting up in the bed.

"What do you mean?"

"Howard, I mean I just don't want to see him."

"Look, don't get yourself all worked up. He wasn't here when I got back from work. He left a note saying he was going for a walk. You were fast asleep. What is it?"

I smiled weakly, knowing I could never tell him what had gone on between Howard and me even if I wanted to. Mainly because I wanted to get out of this marriage alive – and with our son. And also because I'd just come back from having an affair with Stefan; so no I didn't dare tell him. Just the thought of what Jan would do if he knew made me shiver. So instead I improvised and said, "Look Jan I just don't feel so good and I don't want anybody around. Is that so hard to understand?"

"I know, I know," he patted my hand and smiled, "but Howard isn't just anybody, is he? I mean he's your sister's husband Rachel. He's family. And if anybody should understand how you feel, well he should. He's a doctor, a gynecologist, isn't he? And he knows your father just died and that you're pregnant. The guy doesn't expect you to entertain him."

I felt cold all over.

"You're not telling me he's going to stay here?" I said, hot rage racing through my veins.

"Yes that's exactly what I'm trying to tell you. Look I had a little talk with him after he gave you that sedative. You know what he told me? The poor guy is all broken up because his marriage to your sister in on the rocks. He said he's not sure he can buy that whole status trip he's been into anymore. Isn't that something coming from him? He looks different too, doesn't he?

He's changed, lost some weight or something. I don't know. Anyway, he says he just felt he had to get away from it all, far away. And since we're the only people he knows in Europe, he thought he'd come here for a couple of weeks to get a distance from it all."

"You're kidding Jan."

"No, why should I be kidding?"

"A couple of weeks…" Howard staying in our apartment? I knew if Jan had the faintest idea what was going on he'd kill either Howard or me or us both. I shuddered to think of it.

"Jan," I said, "look, he can stay at a hotel. He's got plenty of money. Christ I couldn't bear having him around here all the time."

"Look Rachel, I can't stand hearing you talk like that. The guy's lonely. It's not a question of money. Give the guy a break. Maybe he could really get his act together and grow up, I don't know. We can't just turn him out. And besides I already said he could stay here."

* * *

The next morning when the alarm rang, I sat up in bed. Jan sat up besides me and pushed me gently back down.

"Don't you remember what the doctor said? You've got to take it easy."

"But Jan, I've got to take Daniel to kindergarten and I want to come over to the shop and help you today."

"No way. The next three or four days, you are going to take it easy. Then we'll see. We can't have you going around fainting all the time, now can we? You just go back to sleep and I'll take Daniel on my way to work. No problem." He kissed me on the forehead.

I buried myself under my down duvet and wondered what to do. In the background, I could hear all the morning sounds.

Daniel and Jan making breakfast. Soon they would be going out the door and I would be left alone with Howard. What was I going to do? I wanted to jump out of bed and tell Jan. But I knew I couldn't. My heart was pounding in my chest.

I heard the front door close and the apartment was silent. They were gone. I looked at the clock, it was only 8.30. I jumped out of bed. I had to get out of the apartment before Howard woke up. I tore open the closet and started pulling out my clothes. Clothes, clothes, anything would do. I had my underwear on and was pulling a t-shirt over my head when I heard the door to our bedroom open softly. I froze.

"I figured you'd try to get away before I woke up," Howard was standing in the doorway, naked under his open bathrobe. He came in and closed the door behind him.

"Howard, this is ridiculous." I was trembling all over.

"Really? Well why didn't you tell Jan yesterday? Well?"

What could I say? I looked down at the floor.

"Or would you like me to tell him? Is that it? Would you like me to tell him how I fucked you in New York, how YOU let me fuck you in New York? Is that it? I'm sure I could explain it to him very nicely. Is that what you want?" He walked over to me and took my chin in his hand. "Because if that's what you want, I am sure I can take care of it for you. What do you think your dear husband will say to all that? Do you think he'd like the idea of me coming all this way just to touch you again? Just to fuck you again... and fuck you good! Do you think he'd like to hear how much you actually liked it?"

"Howard, why can't you just leave me alone?"

"Because I want you and I'm going to have you and there's not a damn thing you can do about it."

"You're really crazy man, sick."

"Sick?" He had this strange light in his eyes. "Sick? Maybe, but let me tell you something Rachel. Are you listening? Are you listening good? You are going to do exactly what I want you to do. Do you understand? Because if you don't, I'm going to personally make sure that Jan knows all the details. And I mean every little detail about how you actually agreed to show me your stuff when you were on my exam table in New York. Do you understand?" His eyes were aflame.

"Howard, are you okay? Don't you think you should talk to somebody about all this?"

"Talk to somebody?"

"Yes… why are you acting like this?"

"Acting? Rachel, I'm not acting. For the very first time in my whole life, I'm not acting. This is the real me. Don't you understand? I've spent 45 years of my life doing what everyone else wanted me to do. 45 fucking years! And now I'm doing what I want for the very first time!"

He took me in his arms. What could I do? He had gone mad and in a way I understood him.

For the next many days, I was his victim, his sex slave. That day in New York seemed to have unhinged him totally. He was now a man who saw before him a whole new world of experiences, a whole new world of experiences with me, he'd been missing and now by golly he was going to have them.

So every morning as soon as Jan and Daniel left, he would be standing in the doorway of my bedroom. And each day his desires and fantasies became bolder. And if I was stiff and cold and unwilling to begin with, he would threaten me with telling Jan. Then he would start touching me and licking me all over. And the worst part of it all was that as much as I disliked him, and hated what he was doing, and didn't want him touching me, I always reached a point where I was unwillingly drawn into his passion. And he knew it would happen. He knew that at some point I wouldn't be able to resist him anymore so he would wait and watch and touch me and do things to me over and over again until he knew he had me. And then when I finally surrendered, he knew I would follow him through orgasm after orgasm. In the end, I was so confused and excited and emotionally exhausted that I found myself inhabiting some wild, weird dreamlike state.

I stopped speaking to him completely.

And each morning when he was finally satisfied, he would leave the room without a word and I would go back to sleep. The sleep of the living dead. And then I wouldn't see him again until evening when he would come back and entertain Jan with stories of what he'd done in Amsterdam all day.

On the evening, or should I say night of the third or fourth day that Howard was there, Jan wanted to have sex. He started touching me, fondling my breasts, doing the things he usually did when he wanted me. But I was so exhausted and overwhelmed by what was happening with Howard I just didn't feel I could handle more, so I said as sweetly and as softly as I could, "Oh Jan, I'm just so tired... couldn't we just wait?"

"Wait? Wait for what?" His voice was icy cold.

I held my breath, he sounded so angry.

"You never want it with me you bitch and you know it." He sat up in the bed and shook me. He was pissed. "Are you screwing around again? Because if you are, I swear to God you'll regret it... I swear you'll never see your son again! I promise you that!"

"Oh Jan no!" I cried, "What makes you think that?"

"You're always so distant and you never want to have sex with me... never! What, aren't I as good as Stefan was? Is that it? Tell me you bitch! Tell me!"

He was shaking me, in a rage. That was when I smelt the alcohol on his breath. It made my blood curdle. I'd seen Jan go crazy before when he was drunk so I trembled at the thought of what drinking would do to him now if he felt rejected... I had to get out of this relationship, but this wasn't the time. He was too worked up, too furious.

"Now come here woman!"

He pulled out his stiff cock and pointed it in my direction. "Come here!"

There was no denying him so I pulled myself up and took his pulsing penis in my mouth. I had to calm him down, especially now that I knew he'd been drinking. Otherwise I was sure he'd turn violent. I could just feel it in my bones. So I began caressing him the way I knew he liked it, holding his balls and inserting my fingers deep in his ass. He moaned and grabbed my hair and held me tight to him. I almost gagged his penis was so far into my mouth, but his need was so great there was no turning back. He pounded himself into me, holding my fingers hard up his ass, until he exploded in my mouth.

When he was done, all he did was mutter, "Bitch!" and fall fast asleep.

I shuddered with relief but couldn't help think what would happen if he discovered what was going on with Howard. I had to get out of there – but how? What about my son? I wasn't going to leave without him!

I didn't know what to do and fell into an exhausted sleep.

The next morning, Howard was standing there again in the bedroom door only seconds after Jan and Daniel left. As usual his bathrobe was open and his naked body gleamed in the morning light. His visible sex was pulsing and rising as he stood and contemplated me. I had to admit Howard's sudden change of life had done wonders for his looks. Then I noticed he was holding a tight coil of rope in his hands.

"Howard," I said trying to be very tactful, "there are so many women in the world who would love to be with a man like you."

He didn't reply but kept twisting the rope in his hands.

"Haven't you noticed all the beautiful women here in Amsterdam? I bet quite a few would give their right arm to land an American doctor like you!"

He still didn't say anything. Instead he turned and abruptly left the room. I wondered what was going on. Then he returned with one of the wooden chairs from the kitchen. He placed the chair in the center of the bedroom.

"Take off your robe Rachel, and sit on the chair."

"Howard, didn't you hear what I said? Why does it have to be me? What's so special about me Howard? Howard??" I was hysterical.

Howard seemed so very calm, but I knew that under the surface he was boiling with passion. I sensed that I had to tread carefully.

"Shut up and sit on the chair like I said." He was twisting the rope in his hands.

"Howard, I don't want to sit on the chair. I want you to listen to me. I don't want you to touch me anymore." I was crying. "I want you to go away and leave me alone. Right now!"

He slapped my face. I froze and felt the icy fear creeping up my back.

The man really was crazy.

I fumbled with the belt of my bathrobe and untied it. When I was naked he pushed me down on the chair.

"Give me your hands," he said, standing behind the chair. He tied my hands securely to the back of the chair. The bonds were tight. That seemed to please him no end. He began stroking my naked body, his hands everywhere. I bite my lower lip, sitting there, open and exposed. He moved away and surveyed me and the scene. He seemed very pleased indeed. He walked around the chair then stood in front of me and stuck his stiff penis in my mouth.

"Suck woman!" he said frantically. "Damn it, suck!"

I did as he commanded and he moaned as he thrust himself back and forth in my mouth. But he didn't come, instead pulled himself away just before he was about to climax, his penis pulsing in my face. Then he squatted down before me and spread my legs with his hands, pulling me forward towards him so he could bury his head between my legs. He began licking the tender lips of my vagina. I moaned as his tongue touched me, awakening my sleeping pussy.

At that very moment, the door to the bedroom burst open and Jan was standing there. He was white with shock and still as if turned to stone. I felt hot tears spring out at the corners of my eyes. Then I saw Jan was moving through the room towards Howard who was buried in my pussy and not yet aware of what was going on. It seemed as if everything was happening in slow motion.

"So this is how you repay my hospitality!" Jan bellowed as he flew through the dense, steamy air of our bedroom. He grabbed Howard by the back of the neck and ripped him up and away from me. He raised Howard up and turned him around all in one fluid motion. Howard went limp with surprise and shock. Jan hit him in the face with his fist and blood sprouted from his nose. Howard let out a wail of pain and fell to the floor. Jan caught him with his knee on the way down and Howard groaned again. Jan punched him again before letting him drop to the floor.

"Stop!" I screamed, "You'll kill him!"

Jan seemed to wake up. He wiped his mouth, looked at me and then back at Howard who was sprawled on the floor, his nose bleeding.

"Get up you bastard," Jan kicked him in the side. "Get up before I really do kill you." Jan was heaving him by his arm. Howard struggled to his knees. Jan kept on pulling him. "Come on you bastard. Come on!" Jan dragged him out of the room. My heart was pounding like a drum in my chest but I couldn't move; I was still tied to the chair. I heard Jan shouting at Howard, ordering him to get his pants and shirt on. Howard sniveled and begged but Jan was in a rage.

"And take your fucking suitcase with you, you bastard!" Jan shouted. I could hear him kicking and shoving Howard through the living room towards the front door. "I promise you," he bellowed, "if I ever catch you around my wife again, I'll kill you.

I swear to God I will!" Finally the door slammed and the apartment was silent.

I was in shock, trembling all over. Jan had saved me, but where was he? Where was Jan? Why didn't he come back and free me? Then I froze, realizing how it might look to Jan. Maybe he thought I was enjoying myself, maybe he thought I had agreed to all this. Jan didn't understand a thing. Where was he? The apartment was silent.

When I looked up from my reverie, I realized in horror that Jan was standing there, leaning against the door jam, smoking a cigarette. He was staring at me with the strangest look in his eyes. I felt myself turn to stone, paralyzed with fear remembering what he'd said to me the night before.

The clock ticked loudly by the side of the bed. I wanted to speak but I couldn't.

Jan walked into the room and threw his cigarette into the ashtray.

"So you like this stuff, eh bitch?" He grabbed my long hair and coiled it ropelike in his hand and pulled my head backwards. "If you like it so much, why am I denying myself such pleasure?" He jerked my head further back and looked me right in the eye, "If you've married a slut, why waste your time treating her like a princess?"

"It's not like you think Jan, it's not." I found I could speak, but he didn't let go of my hair. His eyes were burning holes in me.

"It's not, eh?"

"No I promise you. Please let go of my hair. You're hurting me."

Hot tears sprung out in my eyes.

He didn't let go and he didn't say anything.

"Jan, he forced me. I didn't want to do it I swear. He forced me."

"Forced you? How could he force you? Why didn't you just tell me?"

"I was afraid."

"Afraid of what?"

"Afraid to tell you."

"Why should you be afraid to tell me? I'm your husband aren't I?"

"I thought you'd leave me if I told you the truth." I started crying.

"Why should I do that?... I should have killed the bastard."

Even if it was too late for Jan and me, I knew I had to tell him the truth.

"Well tell me now, bitch."

"Jan, you're not going to like what you hear."

He tightened his grip on my hair, "It better be the truth." He was livid. He held my face like an angry schoolteacher.

I started with my father's funeral. I told him how I fainted and how my mother arranged for Howard to take me home. I told him everything. How I fell asleep in the car and first woke up in front of his office. The whole time I spoke, Jan didn't take his eyes off me. He didn't move or let go of my hair. I told him how Howard wanted to examine me and how I hadn't suspected anything until I was up on the exam table and Howard had his fingers in me. At this point, Jan let go of my hair and moved his hands down over my breasts. He squatted in front of me and spread my legs just like Howard had done.

"Was it like this?" he asked, wetting his fingers and putting them in me.

I squirmed.

"Well was it?"

"Yes," I replied in a whisper.

"And you like it?" Jan pressed deeper. "Well... do you?"

"Well yes, I mean when it's you... you're confusing me... please stop it Jan. Please!"

But he wouldn't stop it. Instead he kept his fingers in me and started caressing me in the way he thought I liked it.

"Oh Jan, please don't..."

"Oh so you don't like it when it's me.... Is that it?"

I heard myself moaning, but not from desire – from despair.

"Now go on bitch, I want to hear all of it, every fucking detail. So go on." His voice was mean and cold.

"Jan!"

But I couldn't stop him.

And when I didn't speak, he pinched one of my nipples hard with his other hand, hurting me.

"Tell me bitch!"

So I did and he kept caressing me the whole time, asking me for details so I even told him what happened when I got back to my mother's house that night after Kenny overdosed.

"And you just let him?"

When I didn't reply he continued, "Well did you or what?"

"Yes."

"And you didn't put up a fight or struggle?"

"No." I was sobbing, he just didn't understand.

"And when Howard came to Amsterdam?"

"You don't understand Jan, he made me, he forced me... he..." but suddenly I just couldn't go on, "Oh Jan, please stop. You're hurting me..."

"I want to see you come, bitch." His voice was hard; he had that cruel, authoritarian manner. He bent forward and removed his fingers and began kissing me instead, pulling my labia with his lips, inserting his tongue. There was no love in the way he was touching me but still I moaned even though I didn't want it or him. But there was nothing I could do; he simply wouldn't let me go and I was still all tied up. I felt myself swooning with overwhelm and panic. This was my husband, forcing himself upon me and into me. It wasn't supposed to be like this.

I heard myself begging him, "Please Jan, please! Let me go!"

"Go? No way bitch... You do what everyone else wants you to do and now you're going to do exactly what I want you to do..."

And he kept on, bending me to his will until finally I had to let go and come – and I hated him for it. Hated him for degrading and humiliating me the way he did.

After that, he untied me and dragged me over to the bed and pushed me down.

"Please Jan," I cried. "Leave me alone!"

But he wouldn't and he didn't. Instead he took off his clothes and fucked me with a meanness and vehemence I didn't know he possessed. When he was done, I lay there crying while he got dressed. Then he pulled the big suitcase out from under the bed and collected his clothes from the closet, throwing them into it, muttering "Bitch! You'll regret this... I promise you will..." the whole time.

I hide under the covers, just praying he'd just go.

"Bitch!" He kept on hissing as he collected his last few things. Those were his last words, the last words of the man I was married to.

Finally he left, slamming the door after him. As soon as he was gone, I jumped out of bed and ran to the door and bolted it so I was sure he couldn't get back in, even though he had the key.

With the door bolted, I crawled back into bed and slept for hours and hours.

When I woke up hours later, I felt so relieved and grateful. Grateful! They were both gone! Both of them! Gone!

Now it was finally over and I was free.

I got up and called the locksmith to come and change the locks immediately. Then I called my mother and told her I needed her to come to Amsterdam right away. And I vowed to myself Jan would never take Daniel away from me. Ever!

* * *

I was so relieved when my mother arrived in Amsterdam and felt a lot safer. I knew Jan wouldn't dare come around while she was there so her presence was like that of a comforting, guardian angel. But still I was extremely upset and of course I wanted to tell her everything that happened, including the whole sordid business with Howard, but I knew I couldn't. It just wouldn't be right. Howard, after all, was my half-sister's husband – and Marlene was my mother's daughter too so I was afraid my mother would be devastated if she ever found out what happened. But still I was extremely upset and cried a lot. All I could do was attribute my distress to how unbelievably difficult it had been with Jan. She didn't question my story and seemed to think that was more than enough to account for my wretchedness. So the first couple of days she was there, I cried and she comforted me. When I began to calm down a little, we went to a lawyer and I filed for a divorce and for custody of Daniel. With my mother at my side, I had the strength to do it and it all suddenly seemed so much more doable. To my great surprise, Jan didn't even put up a fight for Daniel, probably because in the end he really didn't want the hassle of having a kid anyway. And after all he'd said and the way he'd threatened me! Ugh! But I was so relieved! Suddenly everything was working out and I was going back to New York with my son!

I started breathing a whole lot easier.

As we were packing up my things and getting ready to go, my mother promised me she'd help me in any way she could. She said she'd even send me back to school after the baby was born, if I wanted to go. That really cheered me up and gave me hope. I really wanted to do something with my life after all I'd been through. Some evenings after we'd put Daniel to bed, my neighbor Ginger would join us for a glass of wine and we'd have quite a women's night, laughing and talking about men and such. I started feeling a little better. When I mentioned my fears about the future, my mother would smile and say quietly that I was still young and had my whole life before me. She said there'd be other men. But who, I would reply, would want a woman with two small kids? He'd have to be a saint and I didn't see many of them walking around.

She would laugh and tell me not to worry.

A couple of days before we were scheduled to leave for New York, there was an unexpected phone call.

It was Albert.

Albert!

My heart was in my mouth when I heard his voice. I couldn't believe it.

"What are you doing in Amsterdam?" I asked, flabbergasted.

"Oh just a little business… And how are you Rachel?"

"Well…" I hesitated, trying to catch my breath. My head spun; what should I tell him? How should I begin? After a long pause I said, "Well… in fact I'm packing up to go to New York with my mother and son."

"To New York? What about your husband?"

"Well, we're not living together anymore… we're getting divorced."

"Oh, I see," he said slowly, as if taking in this new information. "Rachel, let me take you to dinner tonight. Then you can tell me all about it, OK?"

"Well… OK…" I replied, feeling faint and hot and cold all over, "that would be nice."

Albert!

"I'll pick you up at seven. I have your address. Stefan gave it to me. He sends you his love… the bum… his wife Monique just arrived in Nice with his two daughters. It seems they're going to give their marriage another try."

"Stefan?" My heart skipped another beat at the mention of his name.

"I'll tell you all about it when I see you." He hung up.

Stefan!

Albert!

I had to sit down.

Albert Giovanni was coming to the apartment! *Albert!* I hadn't forgotten how incredible the man was – or how powerful our connection had been. In fact I had often wondered if he'd just forgotten me or what... Suddenly memories of the intense moments we'd shared came flooding back and I remembered how it felt to be with him when I was in Nice. I trembled at the thought. Oh such a man! And I thought I'd never see him again. And now he was here! In Amsterdam! Coming to my apartment in a couple of hours.

Oh Albert...

I had tried desperately to forget all about him, but now he was here. My mind was in an uproar; my body was in an uproar!

Albert!

But then the thought struck me – what about my mother? How could I tell her about him? How could I tell my mother about Albert Giovanni?

Surprisingly enough or maybe not surprising at all, my mother loved Albert. He walked into my little apartment and swept Isabel right off her feet. He was suave, aristocratic, dark, good looking and obviously rich. He was a man of the world and my mother kept looking at me as if to say – why didn't you tell me about *him* before?

She told him why she thought I should go to New York with her. "Well since my husband died and I am all alone in that big house, why shouldn't I help Rachel now that she is alone? Such a bright, beautiful woman should do something with her life, don't you think?"

"But of course," Albert replied with his most charming smile. "I told her the very same thing when she visited me in Nice. But she was such a serious lady that I didn't think she quite understood what I meant." He smiled at me mischievously, his eyes glowing, "I'm glad to hear she'll listen to you Isabel."

I sat and watched them talk. It was as if I wasn't even there. Why hadn't I thought of it when he called? Albert and Isabel – it was so obvious, they were two of a kind. Both worldly, cultivated and wise. They spoke the same language. And they both looked upon me as if I was some kind of wayward child who'd gone off on the wrong track. (Maybe they were right). But since they loved me, they would indulge me and help me get back on the right track again. Anyway, that was how it felt. And I had to admit I was so relieved when Isabel came to the rescue and seemed to take over my life. I was in such a state of shock after all that had happened that I didn't have the strength to get back on my feet on my own. I knew in my heart of hearts that I sorely needed my mother's help and support if I was going to have a chance of becoming the free and independent woman I so desperately dreamed of being.

Albert took me to dinner at the Grand Hotel where he was staying.

"Your mother is quite a woman Rachel, you are very lucky."

"Yes, I know."

"I went by your husband's shop today."

"How did you know we had a shop?"

"Stefan told me."

"Oh…"

"Your mother is right Rachel. You were wasting yourself here. It's good you're going back to New York." He took my hand in his, looking at it as if reminding himself of how my hand looked. That was when he noticed the ring on my little finger. "What a beautiful ring Rachel. I don't remember you wearing it when you were in Nice."

Looking at the ring brought tears to my eyes.

"My father decided to give it to me, right before he died. So it was waiting for me when I arrived in New York for his funeral."

"There is something very special about it," Albert said, still holding my hand and surveying the ring.

"Yes there is," I said, sighing and looking at it.

Then to my great surprise, I found myself telling him all

about the ring and my father's note. It was such a private matter and so personal, I couldn't understand why I was telling him. But for some reason, it felt right. For some reason, I felt compelled to tell him. That was the effect he had on me; the same as when I was in Nice. There was just something about him, something about his manner, something about the intensity of his presence that made it feel right. It was as if we were still connected, as if we had some deeper bond. So I went on as the tears streamed down my cheeks.

"How very wonderful!" he said gently drying the tears from my cheeks with his soft handkerchief. "The confidence ring! Yes… It's perfect for you," and then he added slowly, "You know Rachel, I just couldn't forget you." I shivered at his words.

Then we sat there in silence for a while. I liked the way that Albert could be so quiet and present, without it feeling strange or forced in any way. I had noticed that about him from the start. But there was also something else about him now too. Something new. I wasn't quite sure what it was, but he seemed changed, somehow different. I couldn't put my finger on it, but I thought he was softer, more thoughtful than I remembered him.

"There's something important I want to talk to you about," he said, breaking the silence, "and I can't do it here. Would you come up to my suite with me?" My heart skipped a beat at the thought, remembering how glorious our past sexual encounters had been. And I had to admit, I still felt wildly attracted to him… He had this power over me, drawing me in, drawing me to him. But there was something more too, something about the way he asked which aroused my curiosity. I wondered what it could be. What could be so important?

When we got to his suite, I stood over by the window looking out over Amsterdam while hung up my coat. He came up behind me and put his arms around my stomach as if it was the most natural thing in the world. I pulled away, turning towards him.

"Are you still pregnant, my dear?"

"Yes. Yes of course. What made you think otherwise?"

"Well it's difficult to see. You're still so thin... and well... women do change their minds..." He smiled and seemed thoughtful, hesitant, which was unusual for him.

"What did you want to talk to me about? Albert?"

He gazed out the window.

"Amsterdam is a beautiful city, it really is... but much too cold. How did you stand it?"

"Albert..."

"Rachel, I must know, could this baby be mine?"

I started to laugh but stopped as the thought penetrated and I realized what he was asking. I was stunned. The baby in my stomach – his child? My mind raced back in time. I'd discovered I was pregnant after I'd been in Nice about a month and a half. Albert made love to me one of the very first nights after we arrived in Nice... So yes, it was possible. Oh my God!

I sat down on the sofa trying to digest the idea. Why hadn't I thought of it before? Slowly I looked up at Albert who was standing perfectly still, looking at me.

"I never thought of it before... never."

He pulled an armchair over and took my hands. He didn't say anything.

"But yes," I said very slowly. "Yes, I guess so... the baby could be yours. But it could also be Jan's or Stefan's."

"I thought so..." he said slowly. "I thought it could be mine."

The room was very quiet. You could have heard a pin drop.

"So walk me through the timeline Rachel will you," he said, suddenly very down to earth and businesslike. "When did you have your last period?"

"August 10th."

"And you arrived in Nice when?"

"August 20th I think it was."

"Now let me see," he was checking his calendar. "Yes, here it is. We met for dinner that very first time on August 24th. Are your periods regular?" he asked very matter-of-factly.

"Yes," I replied. "Like clockwork."

"Well then the night of the 24th when we first made love would have been the perfect time for you to get pregnant," he said slowly.

We were both silent again, contemplating the ramifications of what he just said.

"Yes, I guess so," I said softly.

"When is the baby due?"

"The doctor says May 17th based on me having my last period August 10th."

He took my hand again and said very slowly, as if it was something he'd thought about saying to me for a long time, "Rachel, you know I'm not 30 or even 40 anymore. Life looks different to me now than it did before." I was watching him and he, well he was looking at me with those dark, penetrating eyes of his. "Can you understand that?"

I nodded. Yes, I could understand because life looked different to me now too.

"I didn't really think about it when Stefan first told me you were pregnant. But after you left and went back to Amsterdam, the thought suddenly struck me. The baby could be mine! I kept telling myself it was ridiculous and sentimental of me, but Rachel, I couldn't forget it. I simply couldn't forget it – or you."

I got up and started pacing the room, my mind in turmoil. *Albert Giovanni, the father of my baby?*

"But Albert, what if the baby is born with blond hair and blue eyes?"

He laughed, "Well then at least we'll know for sure that Stefan is the father!"

I went back to the window and gazed out at the city, trying to grasp what was happening.He came up behind me and again put his arms around my stomach. This time I did not pull away but allowed myself to nestle back into his chest.

Then he said very, very slowly, "The truth is Rachel... I am sure, quite sure, this baby is mine."

* * *

Even though I got home early that night, my mother was fast asleep just like Daniel. I went to bed and tried to sleep but couldn't. I got up and paced the room. Damn, I went into my mother. I needed to talk.

"Mother?" I flicked on the lamp by the bed and shook her gently. She woke up easily and sat up.

"Is something wrong Rachel?"

"Well no."

"What time is it?" She was peering at her watch which lay on the little table by her bed.

"Oh it's not late mother, around midnight. But I just have to talk to you. You're not mad I woke you, are you?"

"Why no, of course not! Would you believe it, I think I must have fallen asleep at nine, just after Daniel. That little rascal can sure wear me out." She was smiling brightly at the thought. "Well now that I've had a good rest, tell me what's on your mind. It's about Albert isn't it?"

"Yes."

"What an incredible man Rachel. Why didn't you tell me about him before?"

"Mom, how old do you think he is?"

"Albert? Hmmm... I don't know, late 40s. He's in good shape, but I'd say 47, 48. Why?"

"Oh I was just wondering."

"Wondering if a man like that could be seriously interested in you? Is that it?" When I didn't reply she said, "Well why not Rachel? I mean you're young, you're beautiful, you're bright and very interesting. How did you meet him?"

"I know him better than you think."

"Really?" Our eyes met. "Come on darling, don't tease me like that, it's not fair... tell me."

"You remember when I was in Nice?"

"Of course silly. We met you there so how could I forget? But you were there with Stefan."

"Yes, and Stefan works for Albert."

"So?"

I shrugged and plunged on. "Well mother, the truth is I went to bed with Albert one of the very first days after I arrived in Nice. And now he thinks the child I'm carrying could be his."

That stunned my mother into silence.

And she just sat there.

So I continued.

"And that's why he came to Amsterdam..."

"Oh I see," My mother's voice was barely a whisper now.

"It never occurred to me before tonight when he said it. Up until now I thought that either Jan or Stefan was the father, but going over it tonight with Albert – the timeline I mean – I realized he could be right. He could be the father. And the most surprising part of the whole thing is that he wants to be the father! Can you believe it mother?"

Now my mother was really awake. She threw her head back and laughed heartily. "What a story Rachel! You really are unbelievable!" And then she laughed again and said. "And you might just be one incredibly lucky woman to boot!"

"What do you mean?"

"Mean? Well just think if the baby really is his... Oh I pray to God this baby is his..."

"But mother ..."

"Just think of the life you could have!" My mother was suddenly full of life. "I mean wake up darling. Stefan didn't want you with a baby and you're getting divorced from your husband because you don't love him or want to be with him anymore. And here you are all downcast and feeling sorry for yourself and thinking about the prospect of being alone with two small children… why you even said to me and Ginger the other night that no man could possibly want a woman with two kids… and along comes Albert, a man of real caliber, a mature man of the world who suddenly tells you he wants the baby you are carrying to be his! Well it's like a dream come true, it's like a fairy tale! It really is… Just think about it my dear. What an amazing twist of fate! It's just incredible!"

"But…"

My mother took my hands. "Darling we haven't talked about this before, but is Jan going to help you raise Daniel and the new baby? Can he afford to pay his share? And what about Stefan, what if it's his child? Is he going to help you? Is there anyone you can count on but your dear old mother, and I'm not going to be here forever."

She was right and I knew it.

"And you're obviously crazy about the man! I saw the way you looked at him when he walked in the door and how he looked at you. The two of you simply couldn't take your eyes off each other. And you've already slept with the man and more than once I gather." She knew me better than I thought, "So obviously you must feel something for him. And obviously something's going on between the two of you. He was just drinking you up with his eyes."

"Was he?"

"Oh come on darling… you know he was!" she laughed again.

And I laughed back. "Yes, I guess he was," I said, feeling myself smile inside. "It's true mother, I do find him wildly attractive, obviously… but this is just so out of the blue. I mean I'm just so flabbergasted by the whole thing. I never thought of us being together even if I was wildly attracted to him when I was in Nice. At the time, I mean when I met him, I was with Stefan – or was supposed to be. And well Albert… he always seemed so – well – beyond me. You know... kind of unattainable... The thought simply never even occurred to me."

"Oh Rachel darling," my mother replied, taking my hand again, "I guess it's time to stop underestimating yourself... "

We were both silent, contemplating this amazing turn of events.

Then she added, "Well if it turns out you really do love this man, just think about the kind of life he could offer you and your children. His money can many open doors for you and give you the opportunity to make your life happy and productive, whether it's a good education you want for yourself and your children or a new career path. And based on my first impression of the man, I suspect he'd give you the space to become the independent woman you're dreaming of becoming... he seems mature enough and wise enough..."

When I didn't reply she asked, "How did the evening end?"

"I don't really know... I was so shocked by the whole idea that I told him I just had to go home and digest it all."

"Was he upset that you left like that?"

"I don't think so. He seems different anyway than when I met him in Nice. There he was so glamorous and powerful and sure of himself. Almost ruthless in a way. To be honest, I was a little frightened of him then, but now he seems well... softer and more thoughtful... do you know what he said to me?"

"No what?"

"Well he said that now that he wasn't 30, or even 40, anymore that life looked different to him. What do you think he meant by that?"

"I suppose from what you've told me and from what I've seen that he's starting to feel older and wants to have a family before it's too late."

"He said he'd call me tomorrow."

"Look, why don't we invite him to dinner here? I'll make something wonderful, don't worry! And I promise you I'll find out more about the man! OK?"

* * *

The next day I had to race out and shop. My mother was a great cook and needed all kinds of things for the dinner she was going to prepare. Albert had graciously accepted our invitation and my mother, who was going to make something really special, was quite specific about the items she needed. I had to go racing around Amsterdam to get exactly what she wanted.

Midway through my shopping expedition, I was rushing across the street when I saw Jan and Jeanette in the distance. Jeanette was clinging to Jan's arm. Fortunately for me, they didn't see me so I turned and walked quickly in the other direction.

To think I was married to that man!

I shivered all over and rushed briskly down the cold, windy street.

* * *

After dinner that night, I took the dishes out to the kitchen. It was all part of Isabel's plan. Daniel was sleeping over at a friend's and Isabel wanted me to give her some alone time with Albert after dinner. So she sent me out to make coffee and bring in the dessert. She and Albert settled into my worn sofa for what looked like a very friendly chat.

I took my time. I realized I was still in shock at the thought of Albert being the father of my baby. Why hadn't I thought of it before? Was it because I was so in awe of him that the thought never crossed my mind? Albert? My heart fluttered in my chest and my knees felt weak.

Oh Albert!

When my mother came out to the kitchen she was smiling happily. "Take in the coffee and come back for the dessert."

When I came back she said, "It seems Albert really is quite a mover and shaker in the world of international business...As you know, his company Giovanni International is some kind of heavy machinery, import-export operation, mainly here in Europe. His father started the business out of nothing right after Albert was born and was apparently quite wealthy by the time he died. He left the business to Albert, who is his only son. According to Albert, his operations have grown so fast that today he now also has dealings throughout the Middle East – and not always in the safest places."

"That would explain the Beirut thing," I said, remembering the business about Beirut when I was in Nice. "What else?

"Oh come on Rachel, this wasn't a third degree interrogation! Now let's go in and have dessert. I know he wants to take you out afterwards and I think you should go. Try to relax a little and enjoy his company sweetheart."

Just as I was turning to go she added, "And Rachel, I really do think he's serious about you. I really do."

Then she gave me a big hug and led me back to the living room.

* * *

Albert wanted to get some fresh air and walk after dinner so we walked a bit. But it was winter in The Netherlands and the night air was cold so we ended up back at his hotel, in his suite.

He took me in his arms, but I couldn't relax.

He pulled back and looked at me.

"What is it Rachel?"

"Oh Albert, I'm just so confused."

"Confused about what?"

"About this baby," I said slowly. "What if it isn't yours? What then?"

He smiled kindly and said teasingly, "There you go again!

Worrying! Didn't we talk about this before – when you were in Nice! I was hoping you had learned not to worry so much while you were down there!"

"But this is different!" I pouted.

He laughed.

I couldn't help but smile a little.

"Rachel, if it's any comfort to you, I am absolutely positive this baby is mine." He wasn't joking, he was really serious.

"But how can you be so sure?"

"Oh I don't know… I just know… do you remember the first time we made love?" he said slowly and paused, as if waiting to see how I'd reply.

"Yes," I said, thinking back to that incredible night, "Yes, of course I remember."

"Remember how intense it was?"

"Yes I do…"

"It was as if something happened between us…"

It was true; I remembered how powerful our connection had been and the amazing feeling he had awakened in me that night.

"… and that's why I'm absolutely positive this baby is mine. I just know we made a baby that night."

"Really?" I was having trouble hiding my amazement.

"Yes really, I can feel it in my bones… so if you could just relax a little," he said laughingly, "everything will work out fine. I promise you."

But I just couldn't let it go so easily – we were talking about the baby in my stomach – so I pouted a little more, "But Albert, what if it isn't?"

"See… there you go again. We'll just have to worry about it if – and I mean if – it does happens. But trust me, it won't."

"Oh Albert! You're hopeless!"

"Okay come here and tell me what's really bothering you." I let him take me in his arms.

Snuggled into him it was easier to say what was on my mind.

"I'm just so confused Albert. What does what you're saying really mean? Are you saying you want us to be together and be a couple if the baby is yours? Is that what you're saying?" And when he didn't reply, I continued, "And if that's what you're saying, how would that work? Where would we live? I mean I already have a son."

He was quiet, stroking my hair. After a long pause he said, "Rachel you can have anything you want."

"Anything?"

"Why of course!" He laughed, "Or at least anything I can afford!"

I looked at him and he had this mischievous smile on his face.

"But Albert..." My words faded into the silence. It was nice sitting in his arms. He gave me time, he gave me space. He didn't rush me. In fact, he was giving me an invitation to relax and be myself and tell him whatever I was really thinking and feeling. I knew this was an important moment if we were ever going to be together. It was important for me to be me and to be honest – and not make the same mistake I'd made with other men. So I tried to tell him exactly what I was feeling. "You know Albert, I'm soon going to be the mother of two children – I realize that – but still I want to do something with my life, do something worthwhile, something exciting. I want to make a contribution." It came out in a rush. "Being a mother isn't enough for me."

"Whatever made you think it would be enough for you?" he said, laughing softly. "I certainly don't think it's enough for you, why should you?"

I felt an enormous sense of relief.

"Rachel I'm 48 years old. I'm not 25 and I'm not looking for my kicks anymore – nor am I looking for a servant or a call girl. I've had plenty of both already. You know that. I was attracted to you from the very beginning because you think for yourself. There's something about you that's different. Yes you're beautiful, but you're more than that. There's a depth to you darling... and then... when I asked you back in Nice why you didn't want to have an abortion, you really surprised me by saying something about *the sacredness of life*... That really made an impression on me. That you were so thoughtful... *mindful* I should say... I remember thinking that for all my many years of study and spiritual practice in the East, you were so much wiser than I was and knew so much more. No woman I've ever known (and I've known many) could or would have said something like that. Not a one of them. All of them were – first and foremost – only thinking of their own enjoyment and pleasure. But you, you actually talked about *the value of a life*... So when you said that, well then I knew. Knew how truly special you were, knew you were someone worth being with, someone I could be with, really be with... so tell me why, why would I want to change that now? You know I want a child, and if we can have one together, well that would be wonderful. But Rachel, I don't expect you to do anything except be yourself and do what you think is right."

I didn't say anything but just let his words sink in. Here was a man who was actually saying he wanted to be with me – with me – just the way I was... and not own or possess or control me just to make him feel good. It was a heady experience, something I'd never tried before.

I felt almost safe in his arms. Almost.

"What do you really want to do? Really? Rachel my money can open many doors for you and give you the opportunities you need to make a wonderful life for yourself. You can travel, study, work, do whatever you want. So think big, my dear! Think free!"

"Oh Albert," I hugged him.

After that, making love came naturally.

He felt my stomach and though it was not big, there was the small hardness and the signs of the coming swelling.

He was gentle with me and strangely enough, there was an almost devotional quality to his lovemaking which was such a balm to my troubled soul after what I'd just been through with

Jan and Howard. I felt myself relaxing into his wonderful slow, deliberate tenderness and realized that I'd never experienced this before – not with any man, not even him. Previously in Nice he too had dominated me, and bent me to his will and as exciting as that had been, this was better, deeper and more intimate. It was as if we were – for the very first time – a man and a woman who were beginning to truly know one another and who were about to enter uncharted waters.

I felt a ripple of fear run through me as I let myself open to the gentleness of his touch and wondered if I really dared. And then the thought struck me that perhaps he felt the same, perhaps this was uncharted waters for him too. And then I knew, knew deep inside me that yes it was true; this was uncharted territory for him too. And so I tossed my head and climbed on top of him, laughing and kissing him passionately on the mouth. Our eyes met and I knew he understood, knew he was feeling the same, knew he also trembled on the brink. Did we really dare? Could we really do this? The heart is such a tender offering when it is young and innocent and pure, regardless of one's age.

"Oh Rachel," he sighed rolling over so he again was on top of me, "you are safe with me darling!" And then he plunged himself deep into my womb, touching my most secret places. And I opened myself and let him. Let him take me, let him see me, let him know me.

Yes I felt almost safe with him. Almost.

It was as if the miracle was about to happen.

But I hesitated on the brink.

Reminding myself that perhaps it was a bit too soon for such deep trust. Because there was still the nagging question: Who was the father of the baby?

* * *

The day before my mother and I left Amsterdam, Jan came to see

Daniel. He had Jeanette with him. My mother was there so I felt safe. It was awkward but necessary. He was still Daniel's father. Daniel wasn't really old enough to understand what was happening, but he knew something was going on. Jan and I had been together for almost seven years. There had been love once, but now it didn't work anymore. And you had to move on. That was the way of it, so what more was there to say? We said our goodbyes as politely as we could.

* * *

So I was really going to New York with my mother. Albert didn't seem to expect anything else. Besides, no matter what he did or said, our future relationship wouldn't be clear until the baby was born. And I wanted to live without a man for a while anyway. Some months in my mother's house would give me a chance to relax and think it all through.

Albert promised to visit us in New York. He said he was there quite often on business anyway. Isabel and Albert had become fast friends. She insisted he stay with us in her house on the Island when he came; but he wouldn't consider it. She thought him the perfect gentleman. He accompanied us to the airport on the day we left, making things easier, not giving me time to realize I was leaving my old life in Amsterdam for good. It was mid-December. I was almost four months pregnant.

PART V

NEW YORK

Things became clearer, more final in New York. Since Jan and I were already legally separated, it was only a matter of time until we were finally divorced and I had custody of Daniel. That part of my life was over and sometimes the thought of how the future would be would make me panic and my heart pound frantically in my chest. But my mother was there to talk to and fill the empty space. And Daniel demanded a lot of my time. We put him into a nearby playschool so he had other children to play with.

My stomach was growing now and you could see that I was pregnant – and thoughts of the future filled my head more and more. I couldn't help but wonder if Albert really was the father of my baby. And that made me wonder how I really felt about him. True I was wildly attracted to the man, but did I really love him? Was this love, true love? Was this the real deal? And then I'd get mad at myself for thinking like that. I was going to have this baby no matter what, so what difference did it make who the father was? And I was going to love this baby no matter who the father was. I would make a life for myself and my children regardless, one way or the other. But then I'd think about Albert again and think that if he was so wise and worldly as my mother said, was he really going to be hung up on who the baby's father was if he was really interested in sharing the future with me? If he really wanted to be with me, what difference did it make whose baby it was? It was like I was obsessed with the thought. Sometimes I wished I could just forget the whole matter for a while and rest my tired brain. But I couldn't, so I just went on obsessing and obsessing...

Albert came to New York often and visited us often, but we never discussed who the father of the baby was. In fact, he came to the city so often that he finally rented a fantastic loft in Soho (with an option to buy) rather than stay in a hotel. I soon discovered that the loft wasn't far from the Zen center where he often meditated in the morning when he was in New York. My mother took all this as a sign that he was really serious about making a future together with me after the baby was born. Sometimes I even caught myself thinking – Albert Giovanni courting me! Could it be true? It certainly seemed to be because he couldn't have been more concerned for my happiness and wellbeing. He even started teaching me how to meditate, so we would often sit together like that in his loft on the big cushions he bought. I liked being together in the silence with him, just breathing and being. I liked it very much.

We were together whenever he was in New York, so finally we had time to get to know each other better. My stomach was getting bigger now, so our lovemaking also changed. He was slow and gentle, always being the perfect gentleman and asking me how I felt and what was okay for me. It was a much more heartfelt experience than anything I'd ever experienced with any man before.

Sometimes I had the strangest feeling when I was with him, a feeling quite unlike any other. It was as if time stood still and I felt everything was exactly as it should be. Every breath, every movement, every glance exactly as it should be. And when that happened, I felt there was nowhere else to go and nothing else to do. It was as if it was all done in that moment of time, as if every-thing was perfect, precious and complete. And it would make me shiver all over and I would wonder… was this the dream we've all been dreaming of? Was this it? The real thing? The dream of love? True love? The meaning of life?

And when we shared that exquisite silence, where everything came together into a homecoming more home than home itself, I just knew that God had given me a precious, perfect gift. And when that happened… when I felt like that, then… finally… I felt peace.

Oh Albert!

As I got to know him better, one of the things I found most attractive about him was that he seemed so at ease with himself and the world. And I began to wonder what his secret was. How did he maintain his sense of equilibrium no matter what was going on around him? So one evening, after he'd made slow, tender love to me in his big New York bed, I asked him.

"Albert, how come you're always so at ease with yourself and life?" I said, looking up at his kind, relaxed face, "what's your secret?"

He laughed at my question.

"Rachel, my little miracle, you truly are my little miracle..." he said and fell silent. There it was again, that special silence between us that was always so comfortable and spacious.

I took a deep breath and waited, enjoying his presence by my side.

He propped himself up on his elbow and looked at me and said slowly, "Well I don't know that I am... but if you say so... it may be because I've learned to have a more realistic assessment of the human condition..."

That really got my attention; I loved it when we talked deep like this and wondered what he meant. "A more realistic assessment of the human condition," I let the words roll slowly off my tongue... "Whatever do you mean by that?"

"Well," he said, pausing again and thinking, "I guess what I mean is... I don't expect myself, or other people to be so perfect anymore, which is something I did when I was younger. Now I've come to see and understand that none of us are perfect, that the reality is we're all just human beings, and that we often screw up. It just goes with the turf of being human. So it's easier to relax."

We both laughed and then he continued, "And I've also discovered that even if we do screw up often, it's usually not all that serious. So now I know that if I can just stay calm, breathe deeply, and not go overboard, things will usually work themselves out satisfactorily all by themselves. When you understand this, it makes everything a lot easier!"

I smiled, contemplating what he said. Sometimes he was just so wise.

Then suddenly, the baby in my stomach gave a big kick. My stomach jumped!

"Did you see that?" I said, laughing. We were lying there naked so it was easy to see.

"Yes!" he said, laughing too. He put his hands on my stomach and felt it. The baby was kicking and moving around vigorously.

"Amazing, amazing! Can I listen?"

"Of course."

He bent forward and put his ear to my stomach, listening eagerly.

I stroked his hair. It was nice being together like this. There was such a genuine feeling of warmth, and of closeness and safety...

Oh how I wanted it to be like this... to be us...

But then the thought arose... *what if the baby isn't his?*

And an icy fear gripped my heart...

What if?

So I pulled back again, afraid to really let go and trust.

Trust in life, trust in Albert... I simply couldn't. So instead of really giving myself to him and the moment as I so fervently desired, I kept a part of me back; waiting to see how Albert would be after the baby was born. Sometimes I wished he would just say Rachel I will love you no matter what, but he didn't. Maybe he didn't know himself how he would react if the baby had blond hair and blue eyes so I kept a part of me to myself. Or at least I tried to and tried to cultivate being independent. I didn't want to count on him too much and then have him disappear once the baby was born.

And so the days passed. And our little dance of moving closer and then me pulling back, moving closer and then me pulling back continued.... And sometimes he'd have that special kind, warm, wonderful look in his eyes when he looked at me, and my heart would leap for joy in my breast. And then he'd be off to the Riviera again. And I'd miss him.

One day in late February when he was back in New York again, Albert said, "Rachel, I want you to meet my old sensei. He's visiting New York to give Dharma talks at the Zen monastery in upstate New York. He's very old and frail and this may be the last chance you will have to meet him. It would mean a lot to me to have the two of you meet before he passes away."

I was surprised and touched that Albert asked, and honored that he wanted me to meet his sensei. It also made me realize how little I actually knew about Albert's past. Of course I knew he had a master when he spent time in the East as a young man; he told me that when I was Nice. But he never really told me the whole story or what it meant to him. But now that our paths had crossed again – in such a serious and profound way – of course I wanted to know more about him and understand the role his master and his training in the East played in his life. So his request moved me deeply and I understood that the gesture was a part of Albert's way of courting me and sharing his innermost life with me. For some reason, I was also absolutely sure that he'd never before presented a woman – any woman – to his sensei.

On our way upstate – I think Albert insisted we drive so we could talk – he told me more about his relationship to his sensei and his study and practice of Zen Buddhism. It turned out that he spent four years at his master's monastery in Japan when he was a young man (from the age of 19 to 23). And this, despite his father's adamant opposition. Albert was the only son and his father, who was a very strict and authoritarian person, had expected Albert, as heir apparent, to learn about his father's far-reaching business empire and take over when his father retired or died. Interestingly enough, it was Albert's sensei himself who convinced Albert to go back into the world and become the powerful businessman he was today. Simply because his sensei felt it was Albert's destiny and the way in which Albert could make an important contribution to the spread of Zen Buddhism and meditation in the West. As a result, Albert was using a significant portion of his considerable wealth to support and maintain several Zen centers in various countries around the world as well as the monastery in upstate New York we were heading to. A monastery that was connected to a large rehab center for drug addicts. The rehab center, which was having good results with heroin addicts the world had otherwise given up on, was run by Western monks, all of whom had studied with the sensei in Japan. And that was why the old master was making this visit, to see his disciples one last time.

Finally we arrived at the secluded wooden monastery in the snowy mountains, surrounded by old trees and a profound silence. There was something about just driving up to the place that made me feel awestruck and extremely shy. Albert understood and took my hand and led me carefully inside. One of the young monks greeted us and took us silently to the master's room. There we met Albert's sensei. He was a tiny man – withered and bent like a gnarled old oak tree – but radiating immense strength and power. I felt myself trembling all over, an utter novice in the face of such power and presence.

But he was kind too, and compassionate. And when he stood before me and took my hand, I also knew with absolute certainty that Albert had told him I was carrying his child. He didn't say a word but looked me deeply in the eye and squeezed my hand gently.

And I knew by the serenity I felt that I was receiving a great blessing.

* * *

And so the days passed. Sometimes Albert was there and sometimes he wasn't. Which was fine with me because I also really wanted to see how living without a man actually felt. This was the first time in my life I'd lived without a man. Up until then, I'd always been with someone. I hadn't really thought about it before, but it was true. I wasn't used to being on my own. So it was an adjustment, even though my mother was there to talk to. I was surprised to find I liked keeping my own counsel and enjoyed being on my own, though of course I wasn't sure if I'd have felt like that if I hadn't had my mother around and Albert coming and going. But my mother was good at giving me space, as if she too realized we couldn't be sure how Albert would react when the baby came and she wanted me to be prepared to make my own way. She was so wise in that way, knowing how centuries of condi-tioning made women still believe we were dependent on men even though in today's world we supposedly weren't.

My sister Marlene was also alone and she joined the women's circle at my mother's house. Howard had left her when he came to Amsterdam, but she didn't know he'd been there and I certainly didn't tell her. I was infinitely relieved he wasn't in New York. Marlene didn't seem to know where he was and still hadn't gotten over the shock of him running off to Europe like he did. She had no idea what happened and talked and talked about it. She just couldn't understand how Howard could leave her like that. Suddenly her stable world had crumbled around her and she couldn't cope. Sometimes I cringed inside thinking what would happen if she (or my mother) ever found out what really happened between Howard and me. Just the thought of it made my blood turn cold. It would be such an unbearable scandal for our family. But I comforted myself with the thought that no one need ever know.

At other times, I would try to talk to my sister about men and such in just a general sort of way, but it was difficult. She would just freeze up and I got the feeling she felt I was too different from her, too wild, too dangerous. But Isabel, genius mother that she was, somehow managed to balance the conversation between her two very different daughters and comfort us both at the same time. Isabel, from another world, from another generation, from another time and other sorrows, how well she understood us both, how well she comforted us both.

The first time Marlene met Albert, she was so surprised her jaw dropped. It was almost comical to watch. Of course I knew she was astonished by the fact that he was obviously so wealthy and she couldn't figure out how I'd found a man like him. Albert, always the perfect gentleman, pretended he didn't notice and charmed her with his easy Italian ways.

Once after Marlene left, I heard Albert remark to my mother, "Isabel, how could you have two such different daughters?" And when she laughed, he added, "And neither of them is like you – a pity indeed." And I realized that he could have fallen in love with my mother if she had just been a little younger.

I made inquiries about going back to college and it would be easier than I thought. I decided I wanted to study psychology. I had a burning desire to understand what makes people tick and especially what made me tick. I wanted to learn more about why we are the way we are and I thought maybe I could do something worthwhile with an education like that. I thought maybe I could even help other women who were confused like me when it came to love and sex. Albert liked the idea and so did my mother.

But all that would have to wait because I was heavy with child. Spring was in the air and I longed for the birthing and the lightness of my own body again.

* * *

Then one evening in mid-April when there was only four or five weeks left until the baby was due, we were all gathered at my mother's house for dinner – my mother, my sister and Albert and I. This happened occasionally and we all enjoyed it. My sister and I knew our mother loved to invite Albert over because it was her way of showing him how truly fond she was of him; because the truth was, Isabel was extremely fond of Albert. The two of them seemed to have this special understanding and enjoyed each other's company immensely. And besides, my mother was a fantastic cook and always enjoyed pulling out all the stops. So inviting Albert was always a big deal, a big production and Albert, understanding how much it meant to my mother, would always bring some exquisite wine or champagne and lovely flowers for her and me.

On that night, we'd already put Daniel to bed and were settling in for a cozy late dinner. Albert had just arrived with champagne and caviar, which my mother served in her very best crystal glasses and with her finest mother of pearl caviar spoons. We were having a merry time and I'd even allowed myself a little glass of champagne, despite my very big stomach. We all thought it would be okay, just this once – one tiny glass of the most excellent champagne Albert had brought. And besides, we all felt like celebrating, though we didn't quite know what or why. Even my sister Marlene was in an exceptionally good mood and I had the feeling that she was beginning to relax in Albert's company and really enjoy the man. He had a way with her, as he did with most women – they simply couldn't resist him when he turned on the charm. I flushed to think of it… to think of how absolutely charming I too found him. And of course, the fact that he'd invited her to stay at his house on Cap Ferrat for as long as she wanted probably helped more than a little. Because even though we seldom mentioned the matter when we were all together, he knew from my mother that Marlene was struggling to recover her balance and rebuild her life after Howard suddenly deserted her right after my father's death.

"So Marlene," Albert was saying, "have you decided when you want to come to Cap Ferrat? You could fly over with me you know. I'll be going back in a few days for some business, so I can accompany you if you'd like and help get you settled in." He squeezed my hand under the table. "May is just beautiful on the Riviera, the weather is always perfect and there aren't so many tourists. I am sure you'll love it."

I could see my sister liked the idea. It would make it easier for her to fly over with him. She'd never been anywhere on her own before and now that her kids were away at school, she could stay away until the end of June if as she wanted.

"Oh yes Albert," she said and smiled, "that would be just wonderful. I'd love to go with you."

"Good," he said, holding up his champagne glass in her direction, "I'll arrange for your ticket."

And that was when the doorbell rang. Which we all thought was very strange, very strange indeed. Who could be visiting us at this hour? My mother looked at me as if to say *are we expecting anyone?* And I looked back saying emphatically *no!*

She got up and went to the front door while we all sat in silence wondering who it could be.

We couldn't see the front door from the dining room, but we heard my mother exclaim, "Oh my God!" So we all turned to look at she came back to the dining room with the mysterious visitor.

I took one look and felt all the blood drain out of me.

I tottered in my chair.

It was Howard!

Howard!

I felt myself falling towards Albert, who caught me.

"Rachel darling!" he gasped, holding me "are you okay?"

When I didn't reply, he steadied me and said, "Let's get you over to the couch!"

I felt the room spin.

Somehow he got me moved into the living room and settled

into the sofa. My mother was by my side immediately, helping Albert support me and looking extremely worried.

I was one very pregnant woman.

"I'm a gynecologist," said Howard, "maybe I should have a look at her."

That's when everyone turned and looked at our unexpected guest and I started screaming, "No, no, don't let that maniac near me... Albert please!"

The room turned into chaos.

Everyone was speaking at the same time while Marlene stood as if turned to stone, looking in bewilderment from her suddenly returned missing husband to her hysterical little sister. What was going on?

"Don't let him touch me!" I was screaming hysterically.

Albert was holding me, "Now, now, now, Rachel. There's nothing to be afraid of. The man's a gynecologist. Maybe he should have a look at you! We must think about the baby!"

"No, no, no" I was sobbing, "not him... you mustn't let him touch me."

"But Rachel..."

Howard was pushing himself towards me saying, "This is not good.... She might be going into early labor, let's get her into the bedroom... I need to examine her."

"Albert," I screamed, "not him... not..."

"Darling," Albert was saying in his most soothing voice...

And then I knew... knew there was no other way... I had to tell him.

"The man raped me, Albert... raped me!" I was sobbing hysterically.

Albert froze.

Everyone turned and looked at Howard.

"Raped her!" Howard cried, waving his hands wildly in the air and smiling crazily. "Raped her? Why the little whore wanted it... didn't you? You know you wanted it, Rachel, you know you did, you little slut..."

And then, hearing his words, I really did faint.

* * *

When I came to a few moments later, my mother was calling 911 and Albert was escorting Howard firmly out the front door. I felt really woozy and scared and was trembling all over.

Albert was by my side again a moment later, stroking my head. "Help is on the way, darling. Don't worry!"

I smiled feebly – happy that help was on the way. I didn't want anything to happen to the baby! But I was trembling all over, feeling very, very shaky. The ambulance arrived a few minutes later and the paramedics rushed in, put me on the stretcher and rolled me out to the waiting vehicle. Albert was holding my hand the whole time and got in with me. As the ambulance rushed me to the hospital, the ambulance attendant started checking my vital signs. I found myself sobbing hysterically as he did.

"Is my baby okay," I sobbed. "Is it?"

He was listening to the baby's heartbeat with a stethoscope and when he didn't answer immediately I panicked even more. I closed my eyes and prayed. Prayed that the shock wouldn't affect the baby and that I wasn't going into early labor or anything.

Albert didn't say a word, but held my hand tightly, looking very grim.

We pulled up to the hospital emergency entrance and they wheeled me in.

The doctor on duty came rushing out and told Albert to wait in the waiting room. They wanted to check me immediately and make sure the baby was okay. Albert smiled weakly as they rolled me away. My heart contracted. But I knew he wouldn't be alone for long; I was sure my mother would follow us in her car, leaving Marlene at home to look after Daniel.

Oh Albert!

Oh my precious baby!

I shut my eyes as they rolled me away.

I was surrounded by people and it didn't take long for the doctor to ascertain that nothing had happened and the baby was okay. All the baby's vital signs were okay and I had no contractions and hadn't gone into labor. And the amniotic sac surrounding the baby had not ruptured. So all was well! I breathed easier and they called in Albert, who was quickly followed by my mother who came running in after him.

The doctor explained to us that everything looked fine. But since I'd seemed to have gotten a terrible shock for some reason and had fainted, he wanted to keep me overnight, just to be on the safe side. We all agreed it would be a good idea. And then he left with Albert to arrange to have me moved from the emergency ward to a more comfortable, private room in the hospital's maternity wing. My mother pulled up a chair and sat down besides me and held my hand. I began to cry.

"Now, now," she said softly, "everything's going to be just fine, Rachel. Thank God the baby is okay. That's the most important thing."

That only made me cry more. "Yes I know," I said, sobbing, "I'm so thankful!"

And then I remembered Howard.

Howard!

I felt myself shiver inwardly, but I didn't say a word. I didn't dare – and neither did she.

Shortly after Albert returned with two porters, saying he'd arranged for a nice quiet room in the maternity wing where I could spend the night in peace. So the porters wheeled me out, followed by Albert and my mother. The hospital was large so it was quite a little journey, but before long I was nicely ensconced in a quiet private room at the end of the hall on the second floor of the maternity ward. On the way down the hall of the maternity wing, I glimpsed several new mothers with their partners beaming proudly at their newborn babies. It was a lovely sight indeed and very comforting. I found myself sighing softly as they rolled me along.

By the time we were settled in the room, it was almost midnight and the sudden peace made us realize how hungry we all were! My mother said she'd go and find out where you could buy food and see if she couldn't get us some tea and sandwiches. Albert and I looked at her gratefully even though we knew it would be a far cry from the marvelous dinner she'd prepared which we never got to eat.

With my mother gone, it was Albert's turn to sit by my side and hold my hand. He stroked my hand gently and I sensed that he – like my mother – wasn't sure what to say. So he didn't say anything for a while. And I knew he was trying to calm himself and adjust to the new situation. Finally he said, "I'm so thankful you and the baby are okay darling. That's the most important thing. Nothing else really matters."

Hearing him say those words made me cry again. I was just feeling so emotional. Between the shock of seeing Howard again and then the fear that something was going to happen to the baby, I still felt pretty shaky. It had been a harrowing experience. But I felt I should to tell him about it – should offer some explanation.

"Albert, he really did rape me. And more than once..." I said softly, the tears streaming down my cheeks.

"Oh darling, we don't have to talk about it right now. It doesn't matter to me. Not now, not here, not under these circumstances."

"But... I want you to know. I don't want to hide anything from you."

"Well maybe one day, after the baby's born, you can tell me about it if you want to," he said slowly, "but right now... maybe it's best we just let it rest."

"But..." I started to say, but he didn't let me finish.

"Look I just don't want you getting yourself more upset than you already are... we can always talk about it later... after..." but he didn't finished his sentence because my mother came bursting in with two bags – one with sandwiches and the other with cups and a thermos of tea. I sighed gratefully; happy she cut our conversation short and also because I was starving hungry. I had forgotten what hungry work pregnancy could be.

Albert rolled the little table in the corner of the room over to the bed and pulled up another chair for my mother. She unpacked her little treasure and we hungrily ate the sandwiches and drank the tea. It was nice to settle in with the two people I loved most in the world. They made me feel so safe and loved that I actually started to relax a little. When I looked at them both, munching on their sandwiches, I felt my heart in my throat and wanted to tell them how much I loved them both, but all I could say was, "I'm so glad you're both here with me tonight."

And I could tell by the way they smiled, they understood how I felt.

"No need to worry Rachel," my mother said again. "Everything is going to be just fine. You can relax now. Spending the night here tonight is probably a good idea – just to make sure everything is okay. And then tomorrow when the doctor is satisfied with everything, you can just come home again. You still have four or five weeks until your due date."

"I know," I said, trying to sound confident and cheerful. But it was difficult, because for some reason, I still felt uneasy.

When we finished eating, I realized how tired my mother looked. She looked absolutely exhausted; I'd been so concerned with myself and the baby that I'd forgotten how hard it must have been for her, especially considering all she'd been through lately. I could see Albert was thinking the same so I said, "Albert, why don't you drive my mother home – I don't want her driving home alone at this hour."

My mother started to say she could manage on her own, but

Albert cut her short saying, "Of course, let's get you home Isabel... right away."

"But I don't like leaving Rachel here all alone."

"Don't worry, I'll be back in a jiffy," he replied firmly. "And besides, she can probably use a little shut eye herself!" he said jokingly. We all laughed. It was good to relax a little. He made us both feel so safe. So she gathered up her things and prepared to leave. Then she gave me a big hug and her eyes, brimming with tears, said, "See you tomorrow sweetheart. Now you just have a good rest and don't worry about a thing. Everything's going to be just fine."

After they left, I settled back in the comfortable adjustable bed and shut my eyes. I really was exhausted so it was nice to finally be able to relax a little. And to know that Albert would be back soon. He'd already told me he was planning on staying the night with me at the hospital. I loved him so. I had to admit it. I loved him for the way he was there for me, solid as a rock – through thick and through thin.

I sighed happily and dozed off.

And awoke smiling because I heard someone whispering softly in my ear, "Rachel darling, oh my darling Rachel". I smiled thinking how quickly Albert had returned. But when I felt a hand on my breast I opened my eyes because I knew Albert would never touch me like that. Especially not now, after all that had happened.

And it wasn't Albert, it was Howard!

Howard!

It was Howard who was groping my breast!

I froze.

Howard!

How did he get here?

"Howard! What are you doing?" I cried, pushing his hand away.

He leaned forward trying to kiss my lips muttering, "Rachel,

Rachel, I couldn't live without you. I had to find you. Darling Rachel... finally I found you... Rachel..."

"Howard!" I pushed him away from me. "Howard, this is insane. What are you doing here?"

"I am your gynecologist remember! When I saw the ambulance take you away, I knew they'd bring you here. They know me; so I just told them I was your doctor and I wanted to look in on you."

I was now fully awake. "Howard, this is insane," I cried. "Please go immediately before I hit the call button!" I started to raise my hand to hit the button.

"Oh no you don't!" he said, grabbing my hands and holding them tightly in his. "You're not getting away from me this time!" Then he lunged forward and began kissing my neck, moaning loudly.

I struggled to free myself, but he had me in an iron grip.

The man was insane.

"Howard, let me go! I'm eight months pregnant for God's sake!" I shouted, which made him let go of my hands and take my face in his hands and kiss me ferociously on the mouth so I couldn't say more. I tried pushing him away, but he was stronger than me. That was when I tried kicking him away but my legs were under the blanket so it was difficult. And all my struggling just seemed to turn him on all the more because he started climbing up on the bed and positioning himself so he could lay on top of me. I struggled to free myself but couldn't. He was bigger and stronger. And then when I felt the full weight of him beginning to bear down on me and my big stomach, I started screaming at the top of my lungs, "Help, help, help! Somebody please help me!"

I was kicking all I could and struggling with all my might but the maniac wouldn't let me go. Then in a final attempt to escape from him, I managed to wiggle to the edge of the bed and fall onto the floor with him tumbling down on top of me. "Help,

help, help!" I kept screaming at the top of my lungs and that was when I heard footsteps running down the hall.

The door opened and two nurses burst in wide-eyed with surprise followed by Albert who came rushing in seconds after them. He took one look at me lying on the floor and grabbed Howard by the neck, dragging him away from me shouting to the nurses, "Call the police, call the police and get a doctor in here right away!" The one nurse was already by my side because I was lying in a pool of water… my waters had broken in the struggle! Oh my God!

The other nurse hit the panic button on her mobile alarm and two porters came rushing into the room followed by the night doctor.

"Call the police," Albert roared as the two porters grabbed Howard and led him away. Howard kept shouting the whole time they were dragging him out of the room, "You'll never get away from me Rachel… I'll find you… I promise you I will…"

Immediately Albert was by my side. "Rachel darling!" He was stroking my hair and looking at the nurse who was saying, "I'm afraid her waters broke in the struggle. We have to get her into one of the delivery rooms immediately. Help me get her up."

The doctor was down on his knees, saying to the nurse, "What's going on?"

"Our patient's been attacked and in the struggle her waters broke."

"Let's get her down to Room 3 right away!"

They helped me up; the hospital gown I was wearing was soaking wet and I was shaking all over.

"Come Rachel," Albert was saying, "Everything's going to be okay. I'm here now darling. And I promise you, I won't leave your side for a minute."

A powerful contraction hit me; I stopped and groaned, knowing I was going into labor.

The nurse and Albert were holding me tightly.

When the contraction was over, they continued walking me slowly down the hall.

"She's started having contractions," the nurse was saying to the doctor as we entered the delivery room.

They quickly gave me a dry hospital gown, put me up on the bed, and attached me to a fetal monitoring machine. The doctor began examining me. His brow was wrinkled but as soon as he saw the incoming data, he smiled and took my hand and said, "Everything's okay. Your baby's vital signs are fine. So you can relax. But it looks like this little one is going to be born tonight. There's not much we can do now to change that. So you better make yourself as comfortable as you can. For now, I want to keep you hooked up to this machine just a little longer, just to make sure your baby is resting comfortably."

I started to cry and then another contraction hit me.

The doctor watched me with his kind eyes and said after the contraction was over, "I am going to be here all night and I will be checking on you often. Besides the terrible shock you just had and your waters breaking, did this maniac hurt you in any other way? I can call in another doctor if there's anything else we should look at."

When he said that, I only cried more.

So he just sat there and waited until I calmed down a little.

Finally I said between sobs, "No, I don't think so... I just feel really sore and tired..."

"Let me have another look at you," he said kindly and listened to my heart and felt the baby a bit more. "Everything seems quite okay."

Then he continued, "Under normal circumstances, I might consider giving you something to help you relax a little but since you are going into labor, it's not a good idea Rachel. It wouldn't be good for you or for the baby. So I hope the two of you can find a way to settle in a little and relax as much as you can, under the circumstances. You are not particularly dilated yet, so we still probably have many hours ahead of us before this baby is born."

And with that, he took me off the fetal monitoring machine and left. The nurse fluttered around me a bit more and then left too, squeezing my hand saying, "You just press on the call button anytime you need me and I'll be here in the wink of an eye."

Once they left, Albert took my hand and said, "Rachel darling, I'm so sorry, I should have never left you. I didn't realize the man was so disturbed and dangerous."

I began to cry again.

"It's okay darling, you're safe now and nothing is going to happen. All you have to do is concentrate on having this baby. Just think! The doctor said the baby is okay – thank God. That's the most important thing. So now all you have to do is relax as best you can. And I promise you, I won't leave you for a moment."

Another contraction came and went, keeping me silent.

I squeezed his hand.

When the contraction was over, I cried in dismay, "But would you stay if you knew the whole truth!" I didn't want anything to be hidden from this man whom I loved so much. But would he love me if he knew the whole truth?

"What do you mean darling?" he said, looking tired and grim. "I don't care what happened. It doesn't matter at all to me, really it doesn't. All I care about is that you and the baby are okay."

"But it matters to me," I said slowly. "It really does…" I sighed, not understanding why it had to be now, but I just knew it did. I held my belly… wondering how long it would be before the next contraction came.

We were silent for a while and then another contraction came.

There was about five minutes between them now and they were coming regularly.

"Albert, it started at my father's funeral," I said slowly.

"Really darling, you don't have to tell me."

"But I want to. Will you walk me a little? I need to move," I asked.

"But of course." He helped me get down from the bed and we walked slowly around the room. I felt kind of sore all over from the tussle I'd just had with Howard. Just the thought of it made me tremble all over again.

When Albert saw me trembling, he said, "Come, you better lie down again. You need to save your strength for the birthing."

We never talked about Albert attending the birth, but now he was there, telling me with his every move and gesture that he wouldn't leave me for the world.

"Albert," I took a deep breath and continued, "I fainted at my father's funeral. It was a couple of weeks after I left Nice and I'd flown to New York and was pretty exhausted. The funeral was the next day and when we stood around the grave, I just passed out. The guests helped me away from the grave and since Howard was a doctor and my sister's husband, it made sense for my mother to entrust me to his care. He checked my vital signs and took me to his car to drive me home. I was so exhausted, I fell asleep in the car and when I woke up, he had just pulled up in front of his clinic instead of my mother's house. When I asked him what was going on, he said he didn't like me fainting like that and since he was a gynecologist, he wanted to check me – just to make sure I were okay. I was kind of annoyed but agreed, since it made sense. Once he had me up on the table and had checked me, he didn't remove his fingers from me but told me he'd been wanting me all his life. At first I was shocked, but then when I realized the man couldn't have possibly planned it – he didn't even know I was pregnant until I fainted – I thought what the fuck. The truth was I felt kind of sorry for him and to be honest Albert, after what happened that night in Nice with your German friend, I thought to myself, well this is nothing compared to that. Maybe I should give the poor bugger a little pleasure. That's how confused I was. So I let him crawl up on me and fuck me, but when he was done, he wouldn't let me go and wanted more. When I said no he became very agitated and when I tried to leave and he hit me so I ended up with a black eye. I finally managed to escape, but the next evening he was at my mother's house when I came home. I'd spent the afternoon with an old boyfriend who nearly died of an overdose of heroin that very evening, which was a very traumatic experience for me to witness. Kenny – my old love – almost died! It was terrible, terrible to see. So by the time I got home later that evening, I was simply so overwhelmed and exhausted by what had happened since I arrived in New York. I mean my father had just died and then there was the incident with Howard and then Kenny. I remember I could hardly stand up when I got back. The house seemed dark and empty but Howard was sitting there, all alone in the living room, waiting for me. He was immediately all over me, just like today. He had knocked my mother out with a heavy sedative (that seems to be his trick) and sent all the other mourners home because according to him, she was so upset and hysterical. So there was nothing I could do. I was all alone in that house with him with nowhere to run to and too exhausted to fight. So yes, he really did rape me. I was completely at his mercy." I started to cry. "It was awful. He was almost as bad as your German friend."

My story was interrupted by another strong contraction.

Albert was sitting next to the bed with his head in his hands. I'd never seen him like this before. When the contraction was over he looked up and said, "It's all my fault, Rachel. All my fault!" He had this really desolate look on his face.

"Whatever do you mean?" I asked, not understanding what he was saying.

"It's all my fault," he muttered again and then continued, "I should have never submitted you to the degradation you experienced that night with that disgusting man! How could I have done that? How could I have let you?" He got up and started pacing the room. "I've felt guilty ever since that night – the man was such a filthy miserable bastard. And you, Rachel, you're such an angel! What was I thinking? And the way I manipulated you into doing it!" He was really agitated. I'd never seen him so upset before.

"I can't tell you how ashamed I am," he said. And then he added, looking up at the heavens. "God forgive me! God forgive me!"

I was stunned by his words. Stunned and shocked.

I'd never seen Albert lose his cool before.

And then he went on, "I was so jaded before I met you, ruthless in a way you could say... I really didn't care about anything or anyone – not really. I didn't have deep feelings for anyone. That's how bored and cynical I was. I admit it, I do... But then you came along and changed everything for me. There was just something about you darling, something about your sweetness and innocence. I don't know... but somehow you brought me back to life, back to feeling... oh darling! I'm so sorry... so, so sorry. How can I ever make it up to you?"

Another contraction slammed me. I groaned and panted.

"But there's more," I whispered slowly when the contraction passed. "More..."

"Oh no," he whispered, sitting down and putting his head in his hands again. "I don't know if I can bear to hear it, dear."

"You must," I said. "You must." And then I told him briefly what happened in Amsterdam right before he came to visit me. How I'd gone back to Jan because I didn't know what else to do and how Howard came and raped me over and over again. I was in a hurry to tell him because I knew soon my labor would be so intense that I wouldn't be able to speak anymore.

When he lifted up his head to look at me, there were tears in his eyes.

"And to think you were carrying my child, through all of this..." was all he could say. A lone tear rolled down his cheek. He made no effort to hide his distress.

Another contraction.

Silence.

The doctor came in to check me again. Albert made no attempt to hide the tears in his eyes.

The doctor said everything looked fine. "You're quite dilated now Rachel, so it won't be long now. I'll be back shortly," he said and left.

"Albert, please call my mother and tell her to come right away," I said panting. "I promised her she could be with me during the birthing."

"Darling, before you mother comes, there is something I must say."

Another strong contraction. I kept on panting.

"Okay," was all I could manage to say between contractions. They were really coming strong now.

"I want to be with you no matter who the father of the baby is."

There! He said it.

Finally!

He finally said what I'd been waiting so long to hear.

Finally!

But I was too far gone to reply.

And when I didn't, he realized it was because I couldn't. I had moved into the serious birthing zone. He called my mother who came immediately.

And so it happened, I birthed my beautiful little daughter with my mother standing on one side of me and Albert on the other. She came quickly and easily, my little daughter, five weeks before her time. My mother and Albert were ecstatic with the experience and the moment she was in my arms I said to them both, "I want to name her *Isabella* after you mother."

And there she was, in all her perfection – a tiny, ravishing beauty with curly jet black hair and dark brown eyes.

She looked exactly like Albert.

Exactly!

How had he known?

How had he known this baby was his?

He had been so sure, and he was right. She even had a way of curling up her little feet which was exactly like him.

Albert took her in his arms and recognized her immediately.

"Isabella Giovanni! My little daughter!" he said ever so softly as he put his finger in her tiny fist. Her eyes were like deep pools as she looked up into his dark penetrating eyes which were a mirror image of hers.

My mother just stood there in silence, beaming like the angel she was and then she disappeared out the door with the doctor and nurse, leaving us alone to savor our moment.

After a few minutes, I said, "Albert, shouldn't we get a paternity test anyway? So you can be absolutely certain?" I wasn't sure if I was serious or just teasing. But the words just came out.

"No Rachel, let's forget it…" he said, looking me in the eye, "Rachel, you wouldn't have believed me before… but… I've loved you since the day I met you…"

Romance, erotica, sensual or downright ballsy. When you want to escape: whether seeking a passionate fulfilment, a moment behind the bike sheds, a laugh with a chick-lit or a how-to - come into the Bedroom and take your pick. Bedroom readers are open-minded explorers knowing exactly what they like in their quest for pleasure, delight, thrills or knowledge.